THE THREE-ARCHED BRIDGE

THE THREE-ARCHED BRIDGE

ISMAIL KADARE

TRANSLATED FROM
THE ALBANIAN BY
JOHN HODGSON

ARCADE PUBLISHING • NEW YORK

FIRST ENGLISH-LANGUAGE EDITION

Library of Congress Cataloging-in-Publication Data

Kadare, Ismail.
    [Ura me tri harqe. English]
    The three-arched bridge / Ismail Kadare ; translated from the Albanian by John Hodgson. —1st English-language ed.
      p.   cm.
    ISBN 1-55970-368-7
    1. Albania—History—To 1501—Fiction. I. Hodgson, John.
II. Title.
PG9621.K3U713   1997
891'.9913—dc20   96–41236

Published in the United States by Arcade Publishing, Inc., New York

Distributed by Little, Brown and Company

10 9 8 7 6 5 4 3 2 1

BP

Designed by API

PRINTED IN THE UNITED STATES OF AMERICA

O tremble, bridge of stone,
As I tremble in this tomb!

(Ballad of the Immured)

THE THREE-ARCHED BRIDGE

1

I THE MONK GJON, *the sonne of Gjorg Ukcama, know-,
ynge that ther is no thynge wryttene in owre tonge
about the Brigge of the Ujana e Keqe,* have decided to
write its story, especially when legends, false tales, and
rumors of every kind continue to be woven around it,
now that its construction is finished and it has even twice
been sprinkled with blood, at pier and parapet.

Late last Sunday night, when I had gone out to walk
on the sandbank, I saw the idiot Gjelosh Uk-Markaj
walking on the bridge. He was laughing to himself, guf-
fawing, and making crazy signs with his hands. The shadows of his limbs pranced over the spine of the bridge,
stretching down past the arches to the water. I struggled
to imagine how all these recent events might have im-
printed themselves on his disordered mind, and I told myself how foolish people are to laugh whenever they see
him crossing the bridge, bellowing and waving his arms,
thinking he is riding a horse. In fact, what people know

about this bridge is no less confused than the inventions of the mind of a madman.

To stop them spreading truths and untruths about this bridge in the eleven languages of the peninsula, I will attempt to write the whole truth about it: in other words, to record the lie we saw and the truth we did not see and to put down both the daily events that are as ordinary as stones and also the major horrors, which are about as many in number as the arches of the bridge.

Muleteers and caravans are now spreading all over the great land of the Balkans the legend of the sacrifice allegedly performed at the piers of the bridge. Few people know that this was not a sacrifice dedicated to the naiads of the waters but just an ordinary crime, to which I will bear witness among other things before our millennium. I say millennium, because this is one of those legends that survives for more than a thousand years. It begins in death and ends in death and we know that news of death or rumor leavened by the yeast of death is the least likely thing of all to fear death itself.

I write this chronicle in haste, because times are troubled, and the future looks blacker than ever before. After the chilling events at the bridge, people and the times have calmed down a little, but another evil has appeared on the horizon — the Turkish state. The shadows of its minarets are slowly falling over us.

This is an ominous peace, worse than any war. For centuries we had been neighbors with the ancient land of the Greeks; then suddenly, insensibly, by subterfuge, and as if in a bad dream, we awoke one morning to find ourselves neighbors of the Empire of the Ottomans.

The forest of its minarets grows darker on all sides. I

have a premonition that the destiny of Arberia will soon change, especially after what happened this winter, when blood was shed for the second time on the newly finished bridge — this time Asiatic blood. But everything will find its place in my chronicle.

2

A T THE BEGINNING OF MARCH in the year 1377, on the right bank of the Ujana e Keqe, no more than fifty paces from the stakes half-embedded in the ground to whose iron cleats the raft that traversed the river was moored every night, a traveler whom nobody in this district knew fell in an epileptic fit. The ferryman, who had seen everything with his own eyes, said that this unknown vagrant of half-saintly and half-crazy appearance, after wandering along the riverbank for a stretch between the jetty and the spot where the river is fordable in summer, gave out a sudden shriek as if his throat were cut and fell face down in the mud.

Even though this was the spot on the bank where people and livestock crossed the river by raft, it was still a mere backwater, unused to sensational events. Of course such things had happened, as at every river crossing, and especially such a crossing as this, where the ever-changing but ever-constant waters of the river suddenly cut across the ancient highway, which was of such great length that nobody knew where it came from. Yet such events had been rare. Usually, people who gathered to cross the river simply waited as people do at such times, in silence. In bad weather, wrapped in sodden black skins, they mutely watched the swirling, dun-colored waters of the river. Even the harness bells of the horses alongside them had a muffled sound, as did the voices of the small children, who would grow increasingly distressed by the appearance of the raft as it approached, with its hunchbacked ferryman.

A kind of wilderness stretched all around; the low riverbank, sometimes sandy, sometimes muddy, receded into the distance, patched here and there with reeds. There was not the smallest house to be seen; even the walls of our presbytery were not visible, while the nearest inn was some thousand paces off.

There was a metal plaque by the stakes where the raft was moored at night, on which the words "Boats and Rafts" were inscribed in crooked lettering. For many years since such plaques had been put up everywhere, not only in the lands of our own liege lord, Count Stres of the Gjikas, or Stres Gjikondi, as they call him for short, but also far away, even beyond the borders of the state of Arberia, in other parts of the peninsula. This had started in the winter of the year 1367, ten years earlier, when all the rafts used as ferries across rivers, estuaries, and lakes were bought up by a peculiar person who came from God knows where, and whose name nobody knows. They even say that he has no name apart from the phrase "Boats and Rafts," which has sprouted up everywhere like a plant that takes root wherever there is water and moisture. They say that he has the same plaque with the same words even at the great house from which he manages his affairs, and that he even signs the documents of court accounts "Boats and Rafts," almost as if the words were his emblem, just as a white lion with a flaming torch between its teeth is the emblem of our own liege lord.

After this new master bought the rafts and boats, the ferrymen and boatmen became his employees, apart from the odd rare exception, such as the wretched ferryman at the Stream of the Tree Stumps, who would have starved sooner than accept a wage from this damned Jew. Just after the winter of 1367, this metal plaque appeared on our riverbank too, with the tolls for crossing inscribed on it: "For persons, one-half grosh; for horses, one grosh."

In times of drought, when the Ujana e Keqe subsided and ran low, travelers, even when laden with sacks, would cross the river on foot, ford or no ford, to avoid paying the toll. But they were not uncommonly drowned, deceived by the river, which was not for nothing called Ujana e Keqe, "Wicked Waters." Weather-blackened memorial crosses were still visible on both sides of the river. They say that the owners of "Boats and Rafts" were careful to affix such crosses on the bank for every person drowned, with the aim of reminding other travelers what trying to cross the river without the aid of "Boats and Rafts" might mean.

Together with the raft, "Boats and Rafts" also bought the old jetty, a relic of Roman times. Blacksmiths had repaired after a fashion its bent iron cleats, so that the ferryman could tie his hawser more easily, especially in winter.

The raft brought in large earnings, not only from the passage of men and livestock but from the caravans that

carried from Arberia to Macedonia the salt from the
great coastal salt pans, and especially from the carts that
supplied the Byzantine naval base at Orikum near Vlorë.
There had been detailed agreements dividing this income
between our liege lord and "Boats and Rafts." In fact
there had never been the least hint of a quarrel over this
point, a rare thing on the face of this earth. It seems that
"Boats and Rafts" was always reliable down to the last
penny.

3

A SMALL CROWD OF PEOPLE, both familiar faces and strangers, had gathered round the man who had fallen in a fit. He shook and foamed, as if straining to thrust his limbs right across the Ujana e Keqe, while stretching his neck in the opposite direction. Someone tried two or three times to hold his head, as they usually do in such cases, so that he would not crack his skull in his convulsions, but it was impossible to hold still that half-bald cranium.

"It is a sign from on high," said one of the bystanders. This was a thin man who, when we later asked what his business was, said he was a wandering fortune-teller.

"And what sort of sign is it?" someone else asked.

The man's blank eyes gazed at the trembling victim, then at the surface of the river.

"Yes," he muttered. "A sign from on high. Look how his movements span the waters, and the waters pass on their movements to him. My God, they understand each other."

Those standing around looked at each other. The man on the ground seemed somewhat calmer now. Someone was holding his head.

"And what sort of sign is it, in your opinion?" someone asked again.

The man who said he was a wandering fortune-teller half closed his lifeless eyes.

"It is a sign from the Almighty that a bridge should be built here, over these waters."

"A bridge?"

"Didn't you see how he stretched his arms in the direction of the river? And that his body shook, just as a bridge shakes when a number of carts pass over it together?"

"Brr . . . It's cold," someone said.

The sick man was quiet now, his limbs only occasionally twitching in their last spasms, as if they had wound down. Someone bent over and wiped the foam from the edges of his lips. His eyes were desolate and dull.

"This is a holy sickness," the fortune-teller said. "In our parts, they call it the foaming. It always comes as a sign. The sign can portend evil and warn of an earthquake, for instance, but this time, praise God, the omen was a favorable one."

"A bridge . . . this is strange," the people standing about started saying. "Our liege lord must be told of this." "Who is the lord of these parts?" "Count Stres of the Gjikas, long life to him. Are you a foreigner then, not knowing a thing like that?" "That's right, brother, from abroad. I was waiting for the raft when that wretch . . ." "This must certainly reach the ear of our liege lord. Well, a bridge? To be honest, we would never have thought of such a thing!"

9

4

THREE WEEKS LATER I was summoned urgently to the count. His great house, fortified at every corner with turrets, was only one hour's journey away. When I arrived, they told me to go straight up to the armorial hall, where our liege lord usually received princes and other nobles whose journeys brought them through his lands.

In the hall were the count, one of his scribes, our bishop, and two unknown houseguests dressed in tight-fitting jerkins, in fashion who knows where.

The count looked annoyed. His eyes were bloodshot for lack of sleep, and I remembered that his only daughter had recently fallen ill. No doubt the two strangers were doctors, come from who knew where.

"I can't get through to them at all," he said as soon as I entered. "You know lots of languages. Maybe you can help."

The new arrivals did indeed speak the most horrible tongue. My ears had never heard such a babble. Slowly I began to untangle the strands. I noticed that their numbers were Latin and their verbs generally Greek or Slav, while they used Albanian for the names of things, and now and then a word of German. They used no adjectives.

With difficulty I began to grasp what they were trying to say. They had both been sent by their master to our liege lord, the count of the Gjikas, with a particular mission. They had heard of the sign sent by the Almighty for the construction of a bridge over the Ujana e Keqe, and they were prepared to build it — or in other words he, their master, was — if the count would give them permission. In short, they were prepared to build a stone bridge over the Ujana e Keqe within a period of two years, to buy the land where it would stand, and to pay the count a regular annual tax on the profits they would earn from it. If the count agreed, this would all be laid down in a detailed agreement (item by item and point by point, as they put it) that would be signed by both sides and confirmed with their seals.

They broke off their speech to produce their seal, which one of them drew from inside his strange jerkin.

"We must heed the sign of the Almighty," they said, almost in one voice.

The count, with weary, bloodshot eyes, looked first at the bishop and then at his own secretary. But their gaze appeared somewhat blurred by this mystery.

"And who is this master of yours?" our liege lord asked.

They started off again with a tangle of words, but the threads were this time so snagged that it took me twice as long to comb them out. They explained that their master was neither a duke, nor a baron, nor a prince, but was a rich man who had recently bought the old bitumen mines abandoned since the time of the Romans, and had also

bought the larger part of the equally ancient great highway, which he intended to repair. He has no title, they
said, but he has money.

Interrupting each other, they noted down on a piece of
paper the sums they would give to buy the land and the
sum of the annual tax for the use of the bridge.

"But the main thing is that the sign sent by the
Almighty must be obeyed," one of them said.

The sums noted on the paper were fabulous, and
everyone knew that our liege lord's revenue had recently
declined. Moreover, his daughter had been ill for two
months, and the doctors could not diagnose her malady.

Our liege lord and the bishop repeatedly caught each
other's eye. The count's thoughts were clearly wandering
from his empty exchequer to his sick daughter, and the
bridge these strangers were offering was the sole remedy
for both.

They started talking again about the heavenly message conveyed by the vagrant. In our parts, they call that
wretch's ailment moon-sickness, one of them explained,
whereas here, as far as I can gather, it is called earth-
sickness. However, it is virtually one and the same.
These very names show clearly that everywhere they consider it a superior disorder, or divine, as one might say.

Our count did not think matters over for long. He said
that he accepted the agreement, and gave the order to his
scribe to put it down in writing, in Albanian and Latin.
He then invited us all for luncheon. It was the most bitter
luncheon I have ever eaten in my life, and this was because of the houseguests, whose speech became more and
more tangled, while I had to unravel it for hours on end.

5

IN THE AFTERNOON I had the misfortune to accompany
the strangers as far as the bank of the Ujana. I consoled
myself that I was at least not obliged to translate the confusion that issued from their mouths: *This road bad because non maintain, mess complete. Water smooth itself,
road non, routen need work, we has no tales, has instruct,
we fast money, give, take. Water different, boat move
itself graciosus, but vdrug many drown, bye-bye, sto
dhjavolos. Funebrum, he, he, road no, road sehr guten
but need gut repair . . .*
Fortunately, now and then they shut their mouths.
They followed with their eyes the flight of the thrushes.
Then, seeing the granaries, they asked about the quantity
of wheat and the cattle that were taken to market and the
route they took.
I noticed that as we drew nearer to the river, not only
their desire to talk but their spirits declined precipitously.
As they waited for the raft that was to carry them across,

they did not conceal their terror of the waters. This was evident from their faces, without their saying.

Dusk was falling when they finally left. I stared after them from the bank for a short while. They were explaining something to each other, making all kinds of hand signs and pointing to each bank of the river in turn. It was cold. In the fast-falling darkness, they looked from a distance like a few black lines scrawled on the raft, as mysterious and incomprehensible as their inhuman gabble. And suddenly, as I watched them disappear, a suspicion crept into my mind, like a black beetle: the man who had fallen in a fit on the riverbank, the wandering fortuneteller who had been close by him, and these two clerks with their tight jerkins were in the service and pay of the same master. . . .

6

A S EXPECTED, the news of the bridge to be built over
the Ujana e Keqe spread rapidly. Bridges had been
built now and then in all sorts of places, but nobody
remembered any of them causing so much commotion.
They had been built almost in silence, with a noise of
tools to which the ear became accustomed, because it
scarcely differed from the monotonous croaking of the
nearby frogs. Then, when they were finished, they did
their duty in similar obscurity until they were carried
away by high water, were struck by lightning, or still
worse, until they decayed to the point that a traveler, having taken a first step on the rotten planks, would stand
hesitating to take a second, and turn back in search of a
nearby raft or ford by which to cross. This was because
all these had been wooden bridges, while the one to be
built would be a real bridge with piers and strong stone
arches, perhaps the first of its kind in the whole land of
Arberia.

People responded to the news with a feeling between

15

fear and elation. They were pleased that they would have no more dealings with the disgraceful ferrymen, who were always on the other bank when you wanted them on this one, were sometimes not to be found at all or, even worse, were to be found drunk, with the exception of the most recent hunchbacked ferryman, who neither pestered the women nor drank but was so gloomy in his expression that he seemed to be carrying you to certain death by drowning. The rafts were filthy and damp and spun around in the water, making you want to throw up, while the bridge would always be there, at all times of the day or night, ready to arch its stone back under your feet without swaying or playing tricks. They would have no more trouble with the river either, which sometimes swelled and wreaked havoc, and sometimes sank to the merest thread, as if about to give up the ghost. People were glad that the Ujana e Keqe, which had been such a trial to them, would finally be pinned down by a clasp of stone. But this very thing, besides causing joy, also scared them. It was not easy to saddle a kicking mule, let alone the Ujana e Keqe. Oh, we will see, we will see how this business will fare, they said.

And as always before such events, people began to move more among each other's scattered houses; they even went farther afield, to the Poplar Copse, where few had been since the duke of Gjin had been ambushed there, shortly before the betrothal with the house of our liege lord was broken off. There were others who went to the wild pomegranates by the Five Wells, from where they could indirectly emerge at Mark Kasneci's clearing; they would then roll up their breeches to cross the quagmire and come out at the great highway. There, if the news really was such that they could not keep it to themselves, their legs of their own accord ate up the road down to the Inn of the Two Roberts. There, everybody knew what happened: words took wing.

Among those who were not at all pleased about the bridge and even became hostile to it was the old woman Ajkuna. She prophesied nothing but ill for it. It is Beelzebub's backbone, she said, and woe to any with the audacity to climb upon it!

7

A T THE END OF MARCH, one bitter morning (it was one of the three days that mark the tail end of winter), they again summoned me urgently to the count. I was seized with trembling lest those crazy jabberers had come back. I would have found it easier to interpret for woodpeckers. I was ashamed of myself when, dozing in the cart, I found myself repeating to myself as if crazy the ancient ditty, "Oh March wind, oh brother mine, dry the loudmouths on the washing line." However, this time it was not them but the people from "Boats and Rafts." There were three men; one of whom, tall and pale and with a pointed beard, spoke little. Judging by the respect shown to him by the other two, he was one of the main directors of "Boats and Rafts," and perhaps their great master's deputy. All three spoke perfect Latin. They had brought with them some black leather bags, full of all kinds of documents.

This time the count brought us into his study. Heavy oak bookshelves occupied part of the walls, and I strained my eyes to read the titles of the books from a distance, in the hope of asking for one of them some time, should the opportunity arise.

"We fail to understand what complaint the noble count might have against us," said Pointed Beard, not raising his eyes from his bag. "As far as I am aware, we have always fulfilled every item in our agreement."

Our liege lord's cheeks, pale since his daughter first fell ill, blushed above the cheekbones.

I had acted as interpreter for several conversations between the count and "Boats and Rafts," and I knew well that it was always "Boats and Rafts" that complained about our lord, and not the other way around. There had been continual complaints about the delayed repayment of sums borrowed by our liege lord from "Boats and Rafts" since the time of the unfortunate campaign against the duke of Tepelenë. The bank of "Boats and Rafts" had twice reduced the interest rate, from fourteen to nine and then to six percent, and had finally agreed to postpone the repayment of the loans for five years without interest. They were forced into this against their will, because they did not want to create an open breach between themselves and the count, from which they would emerge the losers, since the count could profit from the quarrel and refuse to pay back a single penny. Most princes did this now and then, and everybody knew that there was no power that could force the count to honor an agreement with a bank, even with one of the largest in Durrës, such as the bank of "Boats and Rafts."

So when Pointed Beard mentioned the question of a complaint, our liege lord blushed, because he thought this was subtle mockery.

"What complaint?" he cried. "Who has been complaining about you?"

His tone seemed to be saying, Have you grown so bigheaded as to imagine I would make the effort to make complaints against endless moaners like yourselves?

The man from "Boats and Rafts" eyed him frostily.

"There is no question of a direct complaint, my noble count," he said.

"Then speak clearly," the count said.

The representative of "Boats and Rafts" stared at him fixedly. His beard, coating the lower portion of his jaw, appeared to carry the entire weight of his head.

"Sir, it is a question of a bridge," he said finally.

"Ah," the count said. The exclamation seemed to escape him involuntarily, and we all — who knows why? — gazed at one another.

"A bridge, no less," Pointed Beard repeated, as if doubting we had understood correctly. His piercing eyes never left the count.

"So that's the problem," the count said. "And what concern of yours is it?"

The "Boats and Rafts" representative took a deep breath. It seemed that he needed something more than air to shape the required words of explanation. He began to speak slowly and, phrase by phrase, stated his opinion with increasing baldness. In the end he put it bluntly. "Boats and Rafts" was against the construction of the bridge, because it severely damaged the company's interests. It was not just that the raft across the Ujana e Keqe would fall out of use. No, it was something extremely serious, which harmed the entire system of ferries, or what the Latins called water transportation, which had used rafts and barges since time immemorial and was now concentrated in the hands of "Boats and Rafts."

Our liege lord listened with an expression of indifference. The "Boats and Rafts" emissary spoke in well-prepared phrases. I was able to translate his pure Latin with ease, and even had plenty of time left over to think about what I heard. The visitor claimed that this stone bridge would be the first injury (his exact words) ever brutally inflicted on the free spirit of the waters. Then others could be expected. Nothing but disaster would come of putting rivers in such horrible chains, as if they were convicts.

The count's eyes became thoughtful, and he glanced at me for a moment. The men from "Boats and Rafts" appeared to notice this, because they leaned in my direction throughout the rest of the conversation. They began to talk about bridges not only with contempt but as if they were dangerous things.

Clearly the demon of the waters, in the person of "Boats and Rafts," was in bitter enmity with the demon of the land, who built roads and bridges.

"Forbid them to set foot on our land," Pointed Beard said, "and we will be ready to make a new agreement with you about the old loans."

Our liege lord studied his hands.

The words "forbid them" were uttered by the man with the black beard with such rage and savagery that he seemed to be saying, Kill them, slaughter them, hack them to pieces, so that it will not occur to the mind of man to build a bridge on this earth for the next forty generations.

Some years previously, a Dutch monk coming from Africa had told me about a deadly struggle between a crocodile and a tiger, which he had seen with his own eyes from the branches of a tree.

"We may even consider the possibility of deferring all your debts, over a very long period," Pointed Beard said.

Our liege lord continued to stare down at the ring glittering on his hand.

"Or indefinitely," the other went on.

The Dutchman told me how for a long time the two beasts, the tiger and the crocodile, had circled each other, without being able to bite or strike a blow at all.

"Besides, is the noble count aware of the nature of the business conducted by the man who wants to build this bridge?" asked Pointed Beard.

"That is of little interest to me," the count said, shrugging.

"Then allow me to tell you," Pointed Beard continued. "He is involved in the black arts."

Three times the tiger threw himself on the crocodile's back, and three times his claws slipped on the monster's hard scales. Yet the crocodile could not bite the tiger or lash him with his tail. It seemed that the contest would never end.

"Of course," our liege lord said, "the bitumen he extracts is black."

"As black as death," Pointed Beard said.

They must have noticed again that shadow of gloom in our liege lord's eyes, because they fell back again on evil premonitions. All three began to talk, interrupting each other to explain that one only had to see those barrels loaded with that horrible stuff to be sure that only wizards could take to such a trade, and alas for anyone who permitted carts to cross his land loaded with these barrels, that leak drops of tar in the heat, sprinkling the roads — no, what do I mean, sprinkling? — staining the roads with the devil's black blood. And these drops of pitch always sow disaster. Now it has become a main raw material for war, and this great wizard is selling it everywhere, to the Turks and Byzantium on one hand, and to all the counts and dukes of Arberia on the other, fomenting quarrels on both sides.

"That's what that tar does, and you are prepared to let it pass right through your lands. It brings death. Grief."

But in one of the crocodile's furious thrashes, the tiger, it seems, discerned his soft, exposed belly. He attacked his enemy again with a terrifying roar. The crocodile lunged to bite him, exposing his belly again. The tiger needed only an instant to tear it open with his claws. Burying his head in his enemy's body and crazed by his blood, he tore through the bowels with amazing speed, until he reached the heart.

The three talked on, but I, who knew our liege lord, realized that he was not listening anymore. Perhaps because they had talked more than they should, they had lost. Although the count seemed to be in doubt for a moment, it was never easy to make him change his mind. The sum of money promised by the road company was greater than the entire profits of the water people. Besides, his daughter had shown signs of improvement since his decision to build the bridge.

"No," he said at last. "We will talk no more about the bridge. It will be built."

They were struck dumb. Two or three times they moved their hands and were about to speak, but they did nothing but close their bags.

The beast of the water was defeated.

8

A WEEK LATER the master of roads and bridges bought the stretch of highway that belonged to our lord. Two other emissaries had been journeying without rest for three months and more through the domains of princes, counts, and pashas, buying up the great western highway that had once been called the Via Egnatia and was now called the Road of the Balkans, after the name the Turks have recently given to the entire peninsula, which comes from the word *mountain*. More than by the desire of the Ottomans to cover under one name the countries and peoples of the peninsula, as if subsequently to devour them more easily, I was amazed by our readiness to accept the new name. I always thought that this was a bad sign, and now I am convinced that it is worse than that.

Now down this road came its purchasers, their clothes and hair whitened by its dust. They had so far purchased more than half of it, piece by piece, and perhaps they would travel all summer to buy it all. They paid for it in fourteen kinds of coinage — Venetian ducats, dinars, drachmas, lire, groschen, and so forth — making their calculations in eleven languages, not counting dialects. This was because the road passed through some forty principalities, great and small, and so far they had visited twenty-six of them. More than buying it, they seemed to be winding the old roadway, so gouged and pitted by winters, summers, and neglect, onto a reel.

The highway was older than anyone could remember. In the past three hundred years or so, almost all the holy crusades had passed along it. They said that two of the leaders of the First Crusade, Robert Giscard, Count of Normandy, and Robert, Count of Flanders, had spent a night at the inn a thousand paces down the road from us, which since then had been called the Inn of the Two Roberts.

Tens of thousands of knights of the Second Crusade had also passed this way, and then the Third Crusade, headed by Frederick Barbarossa, or Barbullushi as our yokels called him. Then came the interminable hordes of the Children's Crusade, the Fifth Crusade, the Seventh and Eighth, the knights of the Order of the Templars, the Order of St. John the Hospitalier, and the Teutonic Order. Very old men remembered these last, not from the time when they were traveling to Jerusalem, but from about forty years ago, when they passed this way on their return to Europe.

A sorrier array of men had never been seen, as old Ajkuna said. Slowly, silently, they rode on their great horses, with breastplates patched with all kinds of scrap, which squeaked, *krr, krr,* as they rode, sometimes dripping rust in wet weather. They were returning northward to their own countries, with that creaking like a lament, leaving trickles of rust on the road like drops of discolored blood. Old Ajkuna said that when they saw the first of their ranks, people began to call, "Ah, the 'Jermans' are coming, the 'Jermans' are coming." One hundred and fifty years had passed since they came this way on their journey to Jerusalem; but the stories about them that had passed from mouth to mouth were so accurate that people recognized the "Jermans" as soon as they appeared again. Very old people said that this was what they were called when they first came — "Jermans," or people who talk as if in *jerm,* in delirium. Yet many people seem to have liked this name, since they say it is now used everywhere. According to our old men, these people have even begun to call their own country Jermani, which means the place where people gabble in delirium, or land of jerm. However, I do not believe that this name has such an origin.

All these things came to my mind fragmentarily as the agreement was being concluded. They paid for every piece, yard by yard, in Venetian ducats, and in the end departed very pleased, as if they had acquired the road for nothing. And so, with muddied hair and filthy clothes, they went on their way.

The Dutch monk had told me that the beast of the land, having gorged himself on the crocodile's heart, left the beast dead under its useless scales and, with bloodied muzzle, wandered off through the grassland as if drunk.

9

IMMEDIATELY AFTER THIS, one cloudy morning, two somewhat bewildered-looking travelers dismounted from their heavily laden mules by the Ujana e Keqe. They asked some children playing nearby whether this river was really the Ujana e Keqe, unloaded their mules, and there and then began to dig pits in the ground, fixing some sort of stakes in them. Toward noon, it was apparent that they were building a hut. They labored all day, and nightfall found them still at work; but in the morning they were no longer there. There was only the ugly hut, rather rickety, its door shut with a padlock.

This aroused general curiosity. Everybody, not just old people and children, clustered around it, peering through cracks and crevices in the planks to see inside. They turned away disappointed, shrugging their shoulders as if to say, "Strange, not a thing inside." Some people examined the padlock, fingered it, while others chided them: "Don't touch it. What's it got to do with you?" Then they shook their heads and left.

Four days passed in this way. Interest was waning fast, but on the fifth day it revived again even more strongly. In the morning people discovered, or simply had a feeling, that the hut was no longer empty. There was no smoke or noise, but nonetheless it was felt that someone was inside. Somebody must have come during the night.

Nobody saw him all that day or the next. A damp mist swathed everything, and people who went to the hut and peered through chinks said that the stranger was huddled up inside, wrapped in fleeces.

He emerged only on the third day. He had a tousled, tightly curled mop of red hair, and pockmarked cheeks. He had the kind of eyes that somehow seem not to allow you to look straight into them. A sick gleam that appeared as soon as you caught his eye would totally confuse you. He walked along the riverbank for a long while, crossed to the other side on the raft, and walked there too, returning to shut himself in the hut again.

For days on end, people saw him wade into the river up to his knees, drive in small stakes of some kind, and lower some things like copper sheets into the water. He would study these carefully and then fill his hands again and again with river mud, letting it trickle through his fingers. Everyone realized that this could be none but the designer, or as they said now, the projector of the future bridge.

He stayed two consecutive weeks in the rough little hut, gloomy and not keeping company with anybody.

People came from all parts to see him, and not only the curious or the idle, who are never in short supply at such times, but folk of all kinds. Men who had set out for market came, women with their cradles in their arms, cheesemakers who smelled of brine, and hurrying soldiers.

They stood on the banks near the black stones and the old jetty and watched the man moving to and fro, wading into the water and climbing out again, then returning to the water with his strange tools, then back to the sandbank where he would bend down and vigorously, almost furiously, scratch figures and sketches in the sand itself.

Even though it was clear from a distance that he was excitable (it sometimes seemed that he could hardly keep one of his own hands from pestering the other), he paid not the slightest heed to the people who watched him for hours on end. He did not even occasionally turn his head toward them. He treated old Ajkuna, the only person who had the courage to go up to him and threaten him, with total unconcern. She struck the ground in front of him two or three times with her stick to make him listen, and when he lifted his head from the scrawls, she cried, "What are you doing here? Are you not afraid of Him above?" And she lifted her staff to the sky. Perhaps he did not understand a word she said, or perhaps he did not care. Nobody knows. What we do know is that he bent his head over his figures once more and did not raise it again.

When people realized that nothing ever distracted him, they talked loudly and expressed their opinions about him and his work under his very nose. "Ah, now he's passing the mud through his hands, and he'll find out what sort of land this is," explained someone. "Because land is like a human being, and can be strong or weak, healthy or sick. It can look fine from the outside but still have an invisible disease. And the land itself can't tell whether what it will carry will be for good or ill, and so he's running it through his fingers, to learn all its secrets."

On they talked, approaching now quite close to him, while he went on as indifferent as before. Nobody exchanged a word with him. The only person who kept company with the new arrival was mad Gjelosh. Without telling anybody, and without anybody understanding how, he silently put himself in the stranger's service. He would wait for him to leave his hut at dawn, and carry his stakes and other implements, taking them to the riverbank and back again. Gjelosh was under his feet all day, and this taciturn redhead, who seemed ready to gnaw off his own fingers whenever work did not go well, accepted the mad boy's company in silence. Gjelosh gazed at him in adoration and cleared away anything that stood in the way of his scribbles in the sand, uttering not a sound in the man's presence. His tongue was unleashed only when the designer returned to the hut. "Eh, Gjelosh," people said, "Show us how your master works." And a delighted Gjelosh would seize a stick and scribble in the ground so furiously that mud and pebbles flew twenty paces off. "That's how he works, vu, vu, vu," he went, wildly scratching the ground.

10

T HE DESIGNER LEFT just as he had arrived, unseen by
anyone. One morning, mad Gjelosh scurried around
the hut, again sealed with its padlock. He brought his
head close to the cracks, peered inside for a long time,
and then ran around the hut again. He apparently could
not believe that the man was not there, and so was looking for some other hole or chink in order to find him.

    This went on almost all day. The idiot's eyes had never
looked so disconsolate.

11

THE RAFT CONTINUED to punt men and livestock across the Ujana e Keqe. I do not know why, but after the decision to build the bridge, I began to notice what sort of traffic went to and fro across the river by raft. On the last Saturday in March, I stood watching near the old jetty almost all day. The weather was cold, with a thin rain that erased from the sandbank the final traces of the departed designer's scrawls. People sat miserably on the raft, huddled against the cold, trying to turn their backs to the bitter wind. The expressions on their pinched faces gave little clue as to why they were crossing the river. Maybe they were traveling because of illness, or for visits, or they might just be on their way to the bank, or in mourning. Almost half the faces among them were familiar, while the others were utter strangers, and it was quite useless to attempt to discover who they might be. A monk's habit or the cloak of a simple icon seller might conceal the Venetian consul on a secret mission to who knew where. Such things had happened.

12

T HREE DAYS LATER I watched the raft again from the porch of the presbytery. Only two goatherds with their animals were crossing. The raft made the journey several times until it had carried the entire small herd to the opposite bank. The herdsmen were wrapped in cloaks like those of all common shepherds, but their tall pointed caps made them look somehow frightening from a distance.

Another day at dawn, I heard through my sleep some distant voices, apparently calling for help, and shouting "Ujk, ujk" — "Wolf, wolf." I leaped out of bed and listened hard. They were really protracted shouts of "Uk, oh U-u-uk." I went out to the porch, and in the dim dawn light I made out four or five people on the opposite bank with a kind of black chest in their midst. They were calling the ferryman. Their shouts, stretching like a film over the swollen waters of the river, hardly reached me. It was a cold, bleak morning, and who knows what anxiety had made them set out on their road before dawn. "Uk, oh

U-u-uk," they called to the ferryman, holding their hands to their mouths like the bells of trumpets.

Finally I saw Uk stagger down to the bank in his stooped fashion, no doubt muttering curses under his breath at these unknown travelers, the raft, the river, and himself.

When the raft drew near the opposite bank and the travelers boarded, I saw that the black object was nothing less than a coffin, which they carefully lifted onto the planks of the raft.

I went back to bed to rest a while longer, but sleep eluded me.

13

T HE FIRST CONTINGENT of men and laden mules arrived at midday on the seventeenth of April. Mad
Gjelosh strode out in front of the muleteers, gesticulating
as if pounding a drum and puffing out his cheeks, drunk
with joy.

The men and mules halted on the riverbank, just next
to the designer's empty hut. There, in the wasteland
among the wild burdocs, they started unloading. This
took all day. By late afternoon the riverbank was unrec-
ognizable. It was a complete jumble; people scurried
about, speaking a language like a thicket of brambles,
amid the piles of planks, ladders, creeperlike ropes,
stakes, cleats, and implements of every kind. There was
so much hubbub that even Gjelosh was taken aback, and
I rather suspect that his initial joy was dampened.

Late that evening, the new arrivals began building
sheds by torchlight. That night some of them slept in the
open, if such perpetual restlessness could be called sleep.
They kept wandering, who knows why, from the bushes

to the riverbank, calling to each other with loud voices and seeming to sing, weep, or groan in their sleep. They went *hoo, hoo* like owls, and threw up exactly over the spot where the toads were. Torches glimmering here and there gave everything the appearance of a nightmare. In fact, the anxiety and sleeplessness they brought with them were the first things they conveyed to those around them. The construction of storage sheds and dormitories went on for several days. It was surprising to see how even such rickety huts could emerge from this clutter. The disorder looked incapable of resolving itself into anything, and it seemed quite incredible that a bridge could come out of it. These road people were as rowdy and dirty as the "Boats and Rafts" people were meticulous and organized in everything they did.

By the end of April two further caravans arrived, but work on building the bridge did not begin until the designer came. Now they called him the master-in-chief, because it seemed that he himself would direct the building of the bridge. Excavations began a long way off and to one side, by the bushes, as if the bridge were to run off in that direction, as far away from the water as possible. The workmen dug all kinds of pits and dead-end ditches. Everybody labored to level the ground, far away from the water, almost as if they wanted to deceive the river: "We have nothing to do with you. Can you see how far away we're digging? Flow on in peace."

The network of pits and meaningless lines grew more elaborate as time passed. Everybody began to think that the master-in-chief was quite simply a little weak in the head and was frittering away the money allotted for the construction of the bridge. People even said it was no accident that Gjelosh made friends with him so quickly. It takes one to know one.

Of course, Gjelosh scampered about all day amid the confusion, puffing out his cheeks, gnashing his teeth, and pretending to beat a drum. Nobody shooed him away. Even the master's two assistants, who were supervising the work, said nothing to him. In contrast to their master, they were garrulous and ubiquitous. One of them was powerfully built, bald, and with abscesses on his throat, which some people said were signs of an incurable disease, while others insisted that they were scars from the torture he had been subjected to in an attempt to extract his bridge-building secrets from him. Those who made the latter guess were again divided into two camps. One group said that he had not withstood the agony and had divulged his secret, and others claimed that he had endured everything they could do, arching his back like a bridge under the pain, and had told his enemies nothing.

The second assistant, on the other hand, was scrawny; everything about him, his head, chin, and wrists, was thin and angular. Later when they often waded into the river mud, people said that the master-in-chief always turned his back on the second assistant as they talked in order not to have to see his horrible shins.

14

WHEN THE HEAT tightened its hold and the Ujana e Keqe subsided considerably, work suddenly intensified around the collection of ditches flanking the river. The laborers extended the trenches one by one as far as the bank itself, and then joined them to the river, whose water now began to flow into them. Seen from above, the channels resembled great leeches, sucking the water from the already enfeebled river.

It took less than two days for the appearance of the Ujana e Keqe to change completely. In place of the gentle play of the waters, thick mud spread everywhere, with a few dull glimmers squinting here and there.

Farther downstream the channels led the water back to the river again, but on the site of the bridge everything was disfigured and bedraggled. Dead fish lay scattered in the mud. Turtles and diver-birds gave a final glimmer before perishing. Wandering bards, arriving from nobody knew where, looked glumly at the wretched spectacle of the river and muttered, "What if some naiad or river nymph has died? What will happen then?"

The old raft was moved a short distance downstream, and the hunchbacked ferryman cursed the newcomers all day.

These new arrivals crossed ceaselessly to and fro through the bog with buckets packed with mud, which so dirtied them that they resembled ghosts. Now not only the river but the whole surrounding area became smeared with mud. Its traces extended as far as the main road, or even farther still, as far as the Inn of the Two Roberts.

The lugubrious, unsociable master-in-chief wandered to and fro amid the tumult of the building site. To protect himself from the sun, he had placed on his head not a straw hat, like the rest of the world, but a visor that only shielded his eyes. Sometimes, against the general muddiness, the rays of the evening sun seemed to strike devilish sparks from his reddish poll. People no longer said he was mad; now he was the sole sane exception in the crowd of strangers, and the question was whether he would be able to keep this demented throng in harness.

As time passed, the river became an eyesore. It looked like a squashed eel, and you could almost imagine that it would shortly begin to stink. Regardless of all the damage it had caused, people began to feel pity for it.

Old Ajkuna wept to see it. "How could they kill the river?" she cried. "How could they cut it up, oy, oy!" She wept for it as if it had been a living person. "Killed in its sleep, poor creature! Caught defenseless and cut to pieces, oy oy!"

She climbed down into the mud to seek out the master-in-chief. "The day will come when the river takes its revenge," she muttered. "It will fill with water and be strong again. It will swell and roar. And where will you hide then? Where?"

Whenever she thought she spied the builder in the distance, she would raise her stick threateningly: "Where will you hide then, Antichrist!"

15

WHILE THEY WERE STILL DIGGING THE PITS for the foundations of the bridge piers, our liege lord, the count of the Gjikas, received a request for his daughter's hand in marriage. The request was very unusual. It came from none of the Albanian or European dukes, barons, and princes, as often happened, but from an unexpected direction whence betrothals and wedding guests had never come, the Turkish state. The governor of one of the empire's border provinces asked for the count's daughter for his son Abdullah (what a terrible name!). The proposal, as the envoys said, was made with the knowledge of the sultan, so it was not difficult to realize that this was a political match. Our liege lord, Stres Gjikondi, had been aloof toward his new neighbors, and now they were trying to mollify him.

For longer than people could remember, betrothals had been like a calming oil poured on the sea of hostilities and divisions among the nobles of Arberia. Of course these things pacified matters for a time, but not for long.

If there was a recent reason for a coolness, people's minds worried at it until the day of the hated announcement: "We have important business." After that, people knew what came: a fracas.

A year ago the count of Kashnjet had asked for the hand of our liege lord's only daughter, and immediately afterward so had the duke of the Gjin family, or Dukagjin as he is called for short, whose arms carry a single-headed white eagle. But our liege lord did not grant his daughter to her first suitor for reasons known only to himself, while the second withdrew his suit after an ambush at the Poplar Copse by unknown persons, doubtless suborned precisely for this task by those old enemies of our count, the Skuraj family, whose princely arms carry in the center a wolf with bared teeth.

Quarrels among the Albanian princes and lords have been hopelessly frequent for the last hundred years. The Balsha family, princes of the north, whose arms carry a six-pointed white star and who in recent years have been in continual financial straits, could seldom agree with the proud Topia family, who have pretensions to the throne of all Arberia. Nor have the Balshas been on good terms with the counts of Myzeqe, the Muzakas, who have added to their old arms a forked stream that is rumored to suggest the springs of oil recently discovered on their lands. Yet the Muzakas likewise have been in almost continual animosity with Aranit Komneni, the powerful prince of Vlorë, even though both families are allied by marriage to the emperors of Byzantium, in contrast to the Dukagjins, Balshas, and Topias, who have forged their marriage alliances abroad, exclusively with the French royal family. Nor have the Muzakas been on good terms with the Kastriotis, whose arms also bear an eagle, though not a white one like the Dukagjins' but a red one with two heads. People say that the dukes of Gjin descend from the marriage long ago of the chieftain Gjin to a mountain sprite, while the Kastrioti family, or Castriothi, as they sometimes write their name, are the only Albanian lords to use antique pearls as their seals. Two years ago there would have been a general slaughter among the men of Dukagjin and the Kastriotis at the wedding of the count of Kashnjet, had it not been for the intervention of Dejdamina, the old mistress of the house.

The lords of Arberia imagined they could settle these quarrels by marriages. But as I mentioned, the alliances thrown across this stormy sea have been merely like rainbows straining to climb a few degrees above the abyss. The marriages of the great Count Topia with Katrina, the sister of Balsha II, of the latter with Komita, daughter of the prince of Vlorë, and of the second brother, Gjergj Balsha, to Marija, the daughter of Andre Muzaka, did not in the least deter the three old princely houses from very soon setting aside the wedding music for the drums of war.

Marriages with foreigners have not been any more successful. From the time when the Albanian prince Tanush Topia, father of the present count Karl Topia, snatched Hélène d'Anjou, daughter of the king of France, from the French escorts who were accompanying her to her wedding in Byzantium, ill fortune has dogged many of the marriages in the land of Arberia. Tanush Topia kidnapped the French princess with inexcusable thoughtlessness, without in the least considering that he was entering into double enmity with France and Byzantium, both of

44

whom were greater and mightier than himself. He lived with the Frenchwoman for five years, and she bore him two children. His father-in-law, the king of France, pretended to forget the offense, and invited the couple, son-in-law and daughter, to Paris, supposedly to be reconciled. He killed them both, and still today, after so many years, whenever I see the Topia coat of arms with its lion crowned with the white lilies of the Angevins of France, it reminds me of a tombstone.

Aranit Komneni's marriage into the imperial house of Byzantium was no less troubled. However, where Tanush Topia's marriage became the cause of a quarrel, here on the contrary a quarrel was extinguished by a marriage. Aranit Komneni's coolness with Byzantium arose over the old naval base of Orikum near Vlorë. Taking advantage of Byzantium's difficult position, the Albanian prince brought to light some old documents proving that the Orikum base, before it had been captured and rebuilt by Rome, had belonged to Illyria, that is, the Arberia of today. Without waiting for the conclusion of diplomatic talks with the empire, he attacked and captured one half of the base, which was defended by a garrison of Scandinavian mercenaries. Byzantium then hurried to offer him a princess as a wife, to preserve at least joint possession of the base and the small imperial private beaches nearby. They say that the Turks have recently been doing their utmost to persuade Komneni to hand over the base to them. They have promised the aged prince fabulous sums, and even a princess for his son, if he will cede to them at least his own portion of the base, in other words one half. Rumor has it that Aranit has insisted that he will not exchange the base for the most beautiful girl on land, because, he says, the base is the most beautiful girl on land and sea alike.

Turks have been appearing more often all over the Balkans. You meet them on the great highways, at inns, at city gates waiting for permission to enter, at fairs, on boats, everywhere. Sometimes they turn up as political or commercial envoys, sometimes as trade missions, sometimes as wandering groups of musicians, adherents of religious sects, military units, or solitary eccentrics. Increasingly you hear their attenuated melodies, heavy with somnolence. Everything about them throws me into anxiety, their manners, their soft gait, their hidden movements inside their loose garments that seem especially created to conceal the positions of their limbs, and above all their language, whose words, in contrast to their soporific songs, end with a crack like a mallet blow. This is something different from the conflicts so far. This anxiety turns into pure terror when I realize that these people are concealing a great deal. There is something deceitful in their smiles and courtesy. It is no accident that their silken garments, turbans, breeches, and robes have no straight lines, corners, hems, or seams. Their whole costume is insubstantial, and cut so that it changes its shape continually. Among such diaphanous folds it is hard to tell whether a hand is holding a knife or a flower. But after all, how can straightforwardness be expected from a people who hide their very origins: their women?

Some time ago, I happened to see one of their military units on its homeward journey after taking part in the dispute between the barons of Ohri and the Muzakas. It was a body of mercenaries who had fought for a fixed period for a fee, under a contract. The Albanian princes, like those elsewhere in the Balkans and the Byzantine emperors themselves, have for some years been calling on Turkish units for use in their squabbles among themselves. This was how they first appeared in the Balkan lands. My flesh crept when I saw them traveling in formation along the highway with that somber pace that all the world's armies have. They are leaving us, I thought, but taking us with them. Their eyes roved covetously about, and I remembered the saying of my father Gjorg that every invasion starts in the eyes.

Who first invited them? I fear that many peoples of Europe will one day ask this question. It will be not a question but a shriek. And no one will answer it. Everyone will try to blame someone else. From now on, the truth becomes shrouded in mist. Almost as if it were wrapped in Turkish silk.

And now it was there from which an offer of marriage came. When the Ottoman envoys crossed the river by raft to visit the count, laden with expensive gifts, they were all charm. Their breeches whispered with the stealthy swish of silk. But they returned despondent, with overcast features. The henna glowed threateningly on their short beards. Our liege lord had not agreed to grant them his daughter. In order not to anger them, he had said that his daughter was too young to be engaged, and besides, had been lying sick for some time. In fact the girl was seventeen, and although her sickness had left her rather pale, she was now completely cured. But it was clear that the count did not desire this alliance at all.

16

A LL THAT SUMMER, day and night, the work of erecting the bridge piers continued. They dug pits for the foundations until they struck bedrock, then began filling them with large stones. These were brought by cart from an old, distant quarry and lowered into the pits with the help of a winch that they called a *çikrik*. Its squeaking did not cease day or night as it lowered sometimes stones slung with stout rope, sometimes buckets filled with mortar.

Lime pits had been dug nearby, and some of the men working on the bridge piers were entirely coated with white. But the color of mud still predominated.

Work proceeded feverishly on the bridge piers. The master-in-chief, with his assistants in tow, spent hours on the wooden scaffolding that surrounded each of the pits. Sometimes they swarmed like demons over the timbers nailed like crosses, and sometimes, when oppressed by the heat, they would plunge stark naked into the river, oblivious to the eyes of the world. They worked swiftly to raise the piers before autumn came, when the Ujana e Keqe would swell. The diversion channels for the river were intended only for the dry season, and after the first rains they would be unable to cope with the volume of water, part of which would flow again in the old bed.

Whenever a cloud appeared in the sky, the master-in-chief lifted his sparkling head anxiously toward the mountains.

In fact, everybody was waiting for autumn to come. Some were curious to see what the river would do when it met the obstacles in its path. Others shook their heads, convinced that the Ujana e Keqe would know how to exact its revenge. It had not earned its name in vain.

People waited for the river to rise, in the way that they wait for someone who has been away from home for a long time, while great changes have taken place in his absence. Although most took the side of the river, and even laid wagers on the scale of its revenge, there were also those who felt pity for the bridge. However, they were still few, and they concealed their sympathy.

The days grew shorter. Summer gave way to autumn without anything noteworthy happening. A workman drowned in a lime pit, and two others were crippled by the winch, but these were very minor incidents compared with what had been expected.

17

Not only gloom-mongers, who always crop up on the eve of disasters, but everyone was in a state of fever. One day toward the middle of the first month of autumn, the river was more turbulent than usual. There had been a storm somewhere in the mountains.

The new waters surged forward like the vanguard of an army, but the diversion channels swallowed them with ease, not letting them flood the works.

It was now clear that the confrontation between the river and the bridge builders was at hand.

Some clear days went by, and then the skies filled with clouds. A thin, penetrating drizzle fell that seemed determined not to leave an inch of the world dry. Wrapped in sleeveless black cloaks, the laborers pressed on with their work under the rain. "How can they not be afraid?" people said. "How can their legs keep them there, now that the river is waking from its sleep?"

Yet the river seemed to bide its time, collecting its strength before attacking.

The diversion channels barely coped with one new onrush of water. But the Ujana e Keqe still did not show its mettle. Old Ajkuna said that the river would play with the bridge like a cat with a mouse. Several more days of rain passed, and now the river's delay was more alarming than any onslaught. Even the builders themselves, coolheaded so far, seemed to grow anxious. A few cold and distant flashes of lightning, like mute heralds, added to the terror. It has sent every sign, people said. Woe to those who fail to realize that.

The river's attack was expected daily, even hourly, but still it did not come. "Oh, 'Wicked Waters' is a good name," people said. "The river knows many tricks and ruses."

And indeed it came when no one expected it. After the days of rain the weather unexpectedly cleared. A blue sky spread itself above, blinding the eyes, and nobody thought that the river, so quiet during the days of rain, could attack now. But it struck precisely at this time.

First a roar was heard, like a thunderclap, and the river at once rushed forward. In a furious onslaught the waters overflowed the banks of the diversion channels and surged into their old bed. In moments there was pandemonium. Pits and clay-packed dykes vanished in the twinkling of an eye. The waters made trash of the planks, beams, pulleys, sieves, and general debris, which were thrown nobody could tell where, and then with re-doubled force hurled themselves against the unfinished stone piers. They carried with them not only tree stumps and stones, but goats, wolves, and even drowned snakes that resembled the emblems and terrifying symbols of an army. They stormed the bridge head-on, were repulsed, lunged from the left, poured from the right, and foamed

51

wildly below the piers. But the stone piers took no notice. Only then did people notice the master-in-chief still poised above the planks stretching from one pier to another, studying the angry surge of the Ujana e Keqe. Some people claim that he sometimes laughed.

It was clear that the Ujana e Keqe had failed in its first contest with the stone yoke they were casting over it. The debris it had swallowed, along with a drunken mason who the waves seized, I do not know how, were not much of a revenge. The water surged on, wilder than ever, and the Ujana e Keqe, colored by the clay it carried, seemed stained with blood.

People looked at the stone teeth planted in the water, and pitied the river. It will rise again, they said; it will recover from its summer sickness, and then we'll see what havoc it will wreak.

But two weeks passed, the river rose still higher, its waves grew stronger, and its roar grew deeper, but still it did nothing to the bridge.

18

T HE SECOND MONTH OF AUTUMN was cold as seldom before. After the first flood, the waters of the Ujana e Keqe cleared and reverted to their usual color, between pale blue and green. But this color, familiar to us for years, now seemed to conceal cold fury and outrage.

The laborers, laden with stones and buckets of mortar, moved like fiends among the planks and beams. The river flowed below, minding its own concerns, while the workmen above minded theirs.

Throughout October nothing of note occurred. A drowned corpse, brought by the waters from no one knew where, collided with one of the central piers, spun around it a while, and vanished again. It was on that very day that there dimly emerged from among the mass of scaffolding and nailed crossbeams something like a bow connecting the two central piers. Apparently they were preparing to launch the first arch.

19

O N THE THRESHOLD OF WINTER, along with the first frosts, wandering dervishes turned up everywhere. They were seen along the high road, by the Inn of the Two Roberts, and farther away, by the Fever Stone. Travelers arriving from neighboring principalities said that they had seen them there too, and some even said that Turkish dervishes had been seen along the entire length of the old Via Egnatia. Sometimes in small groups or in pairs, but in most cases alone, they ate up the miles with their filthy bare feet.

Early yesterday morning I saw two of them walking with that nimble gait of theirs along the deserted road. One led the way, the other followed two paces behind, and I looked at their rags, so soiled by the dust and the winter wind, and asked almost aloud, "Why?"

Who are these vagrants, and why have they appeared throughout the peninsula at the same time, on this threshold of winter?

20

F ROST COVERED THE GROUND. Two wandering bards
had stayed three consecutive nights at the Inn of the
Two Roberts, entertaining the guests with new ballads.
The ballads had been composed on the subject of the
Ujana e Keqe and were inauspicious. What you might call
their content was more or less as follows: The naiads and
water nymphs would never forget the insult offered to the
Ujana e Keqe. Revenge might be slow, but it would come.

Such ballads would be very much to the taste of the
people from "Boats and Rafts." Yet now that they had
lost their battle and the bridge was being built, not one
and not a thousand ballads could help them, because so
far no one has heard of songs destroying a bridge or a
building of any kind.

Since their final departure, defeated and despondent,
the "Boats and Rafts" people had been seen no more.
They seemed no longer of this world, but now the ballads
at the Inn of the Two Roberts reminded me of them

again. Had they given up the fight, or were they biding their time?

Meanwhile the Ujana e Keqe looked more askance at us than ever, or perhaps so it seemed to us because we knew of the stone clasp placed over it.

21

As the season drew to an end, our liege lord invited distinguished guests to a hunt in the Wolf's Wilderness, as he did every year at about the same time.

Besides neighboring lords and vassals, Gjin Bue Shpata, the powerful overlord of southern Arberia, also came. The two sons of old Balsha, Gjergj Balsha and Balsha II, came from the north together with their wives, the countesses Marija and Komita. They were followed by the lord of Zadrima, Nikollë Zaharia, whose arms bear a lynx, and the barons Pal Gropa, lord of Ohri and Pogradec, and Vlash Matranga, lord of Karavasta, as well as another lord, whose name was kept secret and who was said only to be a "man of note in the Great Mountains."

As in every year, the hunt was conducted with all the proper splendor. Hunting horns, horses' hooves, and the pack of dogs kept the whole of Wolf's Wilderness awake night and day. No accidents occurred, apart from the death of a stalker who was mauled by a bear; Nikollë Zaharia sprained his ankle, which particularly worried the nobility, but this passed quickly.

The good weather held. At the end of the hunt, soft snow began to fall, and the snow-dusted procession of hunters on their homeward journey looked more attractive than ever.

Nevertheless, as I looked at them in their order, a spasm seized my soul. The emblems and signs on the noblemen's jerkins, those wild goats' horns, eagles' wings, and lions' manes, involuntarily reminded me of the drowned animals that the Ujana e Keqe had so ominously carried down the gorge. Defend, oh Lord, our princes, I silently prayed. Oh, Holy Mary, avert the evil hour.

The guests did not stay long, because they were all anxious to return to their own lands. During the three days that they stayed in all (less than ever before), we expected to hear of some new betrothal, but no such thing occurred. In fact, the guests held a secret discussion about the situation created by the Ottoman threat.

While the discussion continued, the two countesses, the sisters-in-law Marija and Komita, came to watch the construction of the bridge. It fell to me to escort them and explain to them the building of bridges, about which they knew nothing. They were impressed for a while by the swarm of workmen that teemed on the sand, by the melee, the din, and the different languages spoken. Then Komita, who had visited her father in Vlorë a month before, mentioned the anxiety over the Orikum naval base, and then the two disparaged at length their acquaintances in great houses, especially the duchess of Durrës, Johana, who was preparing to remarry after the death of her husband, and so on and so forth, finally arriving at their sister-in-law Katrina, the darling daughter of old Balsha, of whom they were obviously jealous. I attempted to bring the conversation back to the Orikum base, but it was extremely difficult, not to say impossible.

Under our feet, the Ujana e Keqe roared on with its grayish crests, but neither the river nor the bridge could hold the countesses' attention any further. They went on gossiping about their acquaintances, their love affairs, and their precious jewelry; try as I might not to listen, something of their chatter penetrated my ears as if by force. For a while they maliciously mocked the Ottoman governor's proposal of marriage to the daughter of our count. They dissolved in laughter over what they called their "Turkish bridegroom," imagining his baggy breeches; they held on to each other so as not to fall into the puddles in their mirth. Then, amid fresh gales of laughter, they tried to pronounce his name, "Abdullah," saying it ever more oddly, especially when they tried to add an affectionate diminutive "th" to the end.

22

A T THE END OF THE MONTH OF MICHAELMAS and during the first week of winter, we still saw dervishes everywhere. It struck me that these horrible vagabonds could only be the scouts of the great Asiatic state that destiny had made our neighbor.

They were no doubt gathering information about the land, the roads, the alliances or quarrels among the Albanian princes, and the princes' old disputes. Sometimes, when I saw them, it struck me that it was easier to collect quarrels under the freezing December wind than at any other time.

I was involuntarily reminded of fragments of the conversation between the two dainty countesses, and it sometimes happened that, without myself knowing why, I muttered to myself like one wandering in his wits the name of the "Turkish bridegroom": Abdullahth.

23

ONE OF THE NOVICES attached to the presbytery woke me to tell me that something had happened by the bridge. Even though he had gone as far as the riverbank himself, he had been unable to find out anything precisely.

I jumped out of bed immediately. As often when I heard news or saw dreams, I automatically turned my head toward the mountains. This was a habit left over from childhood, when my grandmother used to say to me, "Any sign you may receive, for good or ill, you must first tell to the mountains."

One could sense that it was snowing in the mountains, although they themselves were invisible. When we arrived at the riverbank, the sight was indeed incredible. As the novice had told me, the builders had stopped work, a thing that had never happened. Those whom neither sleet nor hail, nor even the Ujana e Keqe itself, had succeeded in driving from the bridge had left their work half done and were scattered in groups on the sandbank, some looking toward the bridge, and some toward the river, as if seeing these things for the first time.

As we drew closer, I noticed other people, who had clambered onto the scaffolding and beams and looked like vultures. Among them, close by the recently formed central arch, I recognized from a distance the master-in-chief and his two assistants. Together with the others they crouched by the stone bridge, saying something to one another, bending again, stretching their heads down to study the piers, and then huddling together once more.

"Gjelosh, what happened?" someone asked the idiot, who was hurrying away from the site. "Has the bridge developed a bulge?"

"The bridge, br, bad, very bad, bridge, pa, pa, fright," he answered.

Only a few hours later we learned the truth: the bridge had been damaged in several places during the night. Several almost inexplicable crevices, like scratches made by claws, had appeared in the central piers, the approach arches, and especially on the newly completed span. As pale as wax, the master-in-chief's assistants tried to imagine what kind of tools could have done such damage. The master-in-chief, wrapped in his cloak, stared with a glacial expression at the horizon, as if the answer might come from there.

"But these aren't marks made by tools, sir," one of the masons said at last.

"What?" the master-in-chief said.

"These aren't hammer marks, or chisel marks, or —"

"Well then, what are they?" the master-in-chief asked.

The mason shrugged his shoulders and looked around at the others. Their faces had turned the color of mud.

"The bards," one of them muttered, "a few weeks ago at the Inn of the Two Roberts, said something about naiads and water nymphs —"

"That's enough of that," the master-in-chief howled, and abruptly crouched again by the damaged arch to study the cracks. He looked at them for a long time, and when he too saw that they really did not look like marks made by hammers, picks, or crowbars, he no doubt shivered in terror like the rest.

24

THE NEWS that the bridge had been damaged led folk to appear on both banks of the Ujana, just as in the days after the flood, when everybody hurried to collect tree stumps for firewood.

The surface of the waters was now a blank. People watched for hours on end, and there were those who swore that they had discerned beneath the waves, if not naiads themselves, at least their tresses or their reflections. They then recalled the wandering bards, remembered their clothes and faces, and especially strove to recall the verses of their ballads, distorting their rhymes, as when the wind bends the tops of reeds.

"Who would have thought their songs would come true?" they said thoughtfully. "They weren't singers, they were wizards."

The Ujana e Keqe meanwhile flowed on obliviously. Its banks had been damaged and torn since its unsuccessful onslaught, so that in places it resembled a gully, but it had not hung back. It had finally succeeded in crippling the bridge.

At night, the bridge lifted blackly over the river the solitary span that had been so cruelly wounded. From a distance the mortar and fresh lime of the repaired patches resembled rags tied around a broken limb. With its injured spine, the bridge looked frightening.

25

J UST AT THIS TIME, for two successive nights, a strange
monk named Brockhardt stayed in our presbytery on
his way back to Europe from Byzantium, where he had
been sent on his country's service.

I was reading in the last light of the fading day when
they came to me and said that a person resembling a
monk had crossed the river on the last raft and was asking for something in an incomprehensible tongue. I told
them to bring him to me.

He was very sharp-featured, long-limbed, and unbe-
lievably dust-covered.

"I have never seen such a long highway," he said,
pointing to himself with his finger, as if his journey
weighed on his body like a yoke. "And almost the whole
of it under repair."

I studied his muddied appearance with some surprise
and hastened to explain.

"It is the old Via Egnatia, which a road company is

restoring," I said. He nodded and removed his cloak, shaking dust everywhere. "The very same people as are building the stone bridge."

"Yes," he said. "I saw it as I arrived."

He looked even taller without his cloak. His limbs were so scrawny that if he had crossed those arms of skin and bone, he would have resembled a warning of mortal danger.

"One fork of the road takes you to the military base at Vlorë, doesn't it?" he said.

He must be a spy, I thought.

"Yes," I replied.

After all, what did it matter to me if he asked about the Vlorë base? It belonged to somebody else now.

I invited him to sit down on the soft rug by the fire and laid the small table.

"Sit down, and we will eat. You must be hungry."

I uttered these words in an unsteady voice, as if worried that I would find it impossible to fill all that boniness with food. As if reading my mind, he grinned from ear to ear and said:

"I am a guest. The Slavs say *gost,* and have derived this from the English word *ghost.*" He smiled. "But like every soul alive, I need meat, ha-ha-ha!"

He laughed in a way that could not fail to look frightening. I tried not to look at his Adam's apple, whose movements seemed about to cut his throat.

"Eat as if in your own home," I said.

He went on chuckling for a while, not lifting his eyes from the table. The thought that I had the opportunity of spending the evening with one who knew something about the study of languages gave me a thrill of pleasure.

"And what news is there?" I asked, saving the subject of languages for later.

He spread his arms, as if to say, Nothing out of the ordinary.

"In Europe, you know, war has been going on for a hundred years," he said. "And Byzantium seethes with schemes and plots."

"As always," I said.

"Yes. As always. They have just celebrated the anniversary of the defeat and the blinding of the Bulgarian army. Since then, they all seem to have lost their heads. As you may know, in that country everybody looks for excuses for excitement."

"The blinding of the Bulgarian army? What was that?"

"Don't you know?" he said. "It was a terrible thing, which they solemnly celebrate every year."

Brockhardt told me briefly about the Byzantine emperor's punishment of the defeated Bulgarian army. Fifteen thousand captured Bulgarian soldiers had had their eyes put out. (You know that is a recognized punishment in Byzantium, he said.) Only one hundred and fifty were left with their sight intact, to lead the blind army back to the Bulgarian capital. Day and night, their faces pitted with black holes, the blind hordes wandered homeward.

"Horrible," Brockhardt said, swallowing chunks of meat. "Don't you think?"

It seemed to me that the more he ate, instead of putting on flesh, as he had jokingly said, the thinner and paler he became.

"Great powers take great revenge," he said.

We talked for a while about politics. He shared my opinion that Byzantium was in decline and that the main danger of our time was the Turkish state.

"At every inn where I stopped," he said, "people talked of nothing else."

"And no doubt everybody indulged in vain guesswork over who had first brought them out of their wilderness, and nobody had the least idea how to stop the flood."

"That is right," said Brockhardt. "When people do not want to fight against an evil, they start wondering about its cause. But this is an imminent danger for you too, isn't it?"

"They are on our doorstep."

"Ah yes, you are where Europe begins."

He asked about our country, and it was apparent at once that his knowledge about it was inaccurate. I told him that we are the descendants of the Illyrians and that the Latins call our country Arbanum or Albanum or Regnum Albaniae, and call the inhabitants Arbanenses or Albanenses, which is the same thing. Then I told him that in recent years a new name for our country has grown up among the people themselves. This new name is Shqipëria, which comes from *shqiponjë*, meaning "eagle." And so, our Arberia has recently become known as Shqipëria, which means a flight or community or union of eagles, and the inhabitants are known as *shqiptarë*, from the same word.

He listened to me closely, and I went on to explain to him a Serbian list of names of peoples, with features of totemism, that a Slovene monk had told me about. In it, the Albanians were characterized as eagles (*dobar*), the

Huns as rabbits, the Serbs as wolves, the Croats as owls, the Magyars as lynxes, and the Romanians as cats.

He nodded continually and, when I told him that we Albanians, together with the ancient Greeks, are the oldest people in the Balkans, he held his spoon thoughtfully in his hand. We have had our roots here, I continued, since time immemorial. The Slavs, who have recently become so embittered, as often happens with newcomers, arrived from the steppes of the east no more than three or four centuries ago. I knew that I would have to demonstrate this to him somehow, and so I talked to him about the Albanian language, and told him that, according to some of our monks, it is contemporary with if not older than Greek, and that this, the monks say, was proved by the words that Greek had borrowed from our tongue.

"And they are not just any words," I said, "but the names of gods and heroes."

His eyes sparkled. I told him that the names Zeus, Dhemetra, Tetis, Odhise, and Kaos, according to our monks, stem from the Albanian words *zë*, "voice," *dhe,* "earth," *det,* "sea," *udhë,* "journey," and *haes,* "eater." He laid down his spoon.

"Eat, ghost," I said, staring almost with fear at his spoon, which seemed to be the only tool binding him to the world of the living.

"These are amazing things you say," he said.

"When someone borrows your words for gods, it is like borrowing a part of your soul," I said after a pause. "But never mind, this is no time for useless boasting. Now the Ottoman language is casting its shadow over both our languages, Greek and Albanian, like a black cloud."

He nodded.

"Wars between languages are no less fateful than wars between men," he said.

I was saddened myself by the topic I had embarked on.

"The language of the east is drawing nearer," I repeated after a while. We looked deep into each other's eyes. "With its '-*luk*' suffix," I went on slowly. "Like some dreadful hammer blow."

"Alas for you," he said.

I shook my head in despair.

"And nobody understands the danger," I said.

"Ah," he said, and with a sudden movement, as if freeing himself from a snare, he rose from the table.

He was now free to become a ghost again.

26

T HREE DAYS AFTER BROCKHARDT LEFT, the bridge was damaged again. This time it was no longer a matter of cracks and scratches; some stones in its central piers had been removed. The strangest thing was that some of these stones were dislodged beneath the surface of the water, and this, apart from adding to people's terror, caused great trouble to the builders. It was almost impossible to carry out repairs underwater until the river subsided again next summer.

This second intervention of the spirits of the water caused general horror. Despite the rage of the master-in-chief and his assistants (the designer's head might appear like a bolt of lightning at any part of the bridge), the pace of work slackened at once. Instead of the mud from the building site, terrifying rumors spread out from the sand of the riverbank, which now resembled some blighted plain. But these rumors spread faster and farther than the mud.

Some of the workmen began to abandon their work.

Clutching their bags, and with their wages unclaimed, they stealthily left their work at night, considering it cursed.

Increasingly, people in their interminable conversations began to voice the opinion that the bridge must be destroyed before it was too late.

27

THE BRIDGE'S MASTER-IN-CHIEF left unexpectedly one morning before dawn. Nobody knew where he went or why; it was understood that he himself had given no explanation. On the previous day he had struck his two assistants with a whip of hogshair, accompanying the blows with various strange insults: dog, telltale, liar, mangy cur, arch-asshole. He then threw away his whip and was seen no more.

Work on the bridge proceeded more sluggishly than ever. Gjelosh wandered miserably around the master-in-chief's hut, repeatedly putting his eye or ear to the keyhole. The punished assistants turned up here and there with the whip marks on their faces. One of them, the lean one, was bitterly angry, as outraged as a man could be at the marks of the lashes, while the other man, the stocky one, seemed pleased and seized every opportunity to show off his black welts, almost as proud of them as if they had been a certificate of commendation.

Meanwhile, in the absence of the master-in-chief,

work on the bridge slackened daily. Everybody was convinced that he would never return and that nothing now remained but the decision to pull down the bridge, or at least abandon it to the mercy of the waters.

But the master-in-chief returned as unexpectedly as he had left. A group of official persons accompanied him. They had barely arrived before they went to the site of the damage, where they remained for hours on end. They examined the scratches and the dislodged stones, shook their heads, and made incomprehensible gestures. One of them, to everybody's amazement, stripped off and dived into the water, apparently to inspect the damage below the waterline.

The same thing happened on the second and third days. The inspection team was headed by a tall, thin, extremely stooped man. He seemed to have some kind of cramp in his neck, because he could barely move his head. Judging by the respect shown to him by everybody else, including even the master-in-chief, who was no respecter of persons, people supposed that he must be one of the principal proprietors of the roads and bridges.

"Look how God has bent that cursed one double," old Ajkuna said when she saw him. "That's how he'll twist everyone who wants to build bridges. He'll bend them double like the bridges themselves, so that their heads touch their feet. Our forebear was right when he said, 'May you be bent double and eat your toes, you who stray from the path!'"

28

I WAS SUMMONED in haste to our count. Everyone was gathered there: the emissaries of the road owners, the master-in-chief, and our liege lord's scribes. Their expressions were despondent. We waited for the count to arrive.

I could not at all imagine why this meeting was being held. Would there really be a decision to abandon the works? It would be difficult for our liege lord to pay back even a small percentage of the money he had received. They did not really know his ways.

The delegation sat as if fixed to their high seats. The stooped man who had been so powerfully cursed by old Ajkuna was among them.

These meetings were beginning to irritate me. So in particular was the road owners' garbled language, which made my head ache for two days after translating it. Both sides, the water people and the road people, were equally unknown to me, but at least the water people spoke clearly and precisely. But an hour's talk with the road people seemed to coat the table with the dust of their slovenly language, just as they littered the land where they built.

I will do what I can today, I said to myself, but next time I will find an excuse not to come.

The visitors glanced repeatedly at the door through which the count would enter. In fact, his delay showed that he was not pleased at this meeting. The visitors seemed increasingly on tenterhooks. They stared into space, at their hands, or at some pieces of parchment scribbled with all kinds of sketches.

At last the count arrived. He nodded a frosty greeting and sat down at the table.

"I'm listening," he said.

Evidently the tall, bent man would speak first. He cleared his throat two or three times as if in search of the right pitch and was about to say something, but then hesitated and seemed to abandon the idea.

"I'm listening," I translated for the count a second time.

The head of the deputation also cleared his throat, then said in a dry voice:

"Someone is damaging our bridge."

The count's eyebrows rose. They expressed surprise, but more expectation, and a hint of mockery.

"It is not the spirits of the water who are damaging our bridge, as rumor has it, but men," the visitor continued.

The count's face remained petrified.

The foreigners' representative studied the notes in front of him.

"We may state from the start whom we suspect," he went on.

77

Our count shrugged, as if to say that it was no concern of his whom they suspected. The visitor apparently misinterpreted the gesture, and hastened to add:

"Please do not misunderstand me. We don't suspect your own people in the least." He gulped. "Nor do we even suspect the Turks. Our suspicions lie elsewhere."

"I'm listening," Stres Gjikondi said for the third time.

The scratching of the quills of the count's two scribes made the silence even more painful.

"The 'Boats and Rafts' firm is trying to bring down our bridge," said the foreigners' representative. His piercing eyes transfixed the count. His bent spine put even greater suspicion into his glare.

The count confronted his gaze calmly. It was obvious at once that he was barely interested in this matter. He had been worried all the time about the breach of relations with his Turkish neighbors, and he did not even want to know about what was happening at the bridge.

"It is obvious that they have been and still remain opposed to the construction of bridges, because of reasons that may be imagined, in other words questions of profit," the foreigner continued. "They put forward the idea of destroying the bridge, and then they took action against it. With the help of paid bards, they spread the legend that the spirits of the water will not tolerate the bridge and that it must be destroyed."

His head, bent low over the table, turned left and right to gauge the impression his revelation made on us all. I believed him at once. In fact, I had suspected something of the sort before. If the bridge builders, whose representatives were here before us, could at the very start pay an epileptic and a wandering fortune-teller to be the first to advance the idea of building a bridge, then was it not possible that "Boats and Rafts" could pay two wandering bards to launch the idea of its destruction?

"You must realize, my lord count," the foreigner went on, "that it is not the spirits of the water who cannot endure the bridge but the grasping spirits of the directors of this gang of thieves called 'Boats and Rafts.'"

"Ha, ha!" the count laughed. "They say the same about you."

Small reddish spots appeared on the brow of the leader of the delegation.

"We have never sunk any of their boats," he said. "Nor have we damaged any of their jetties."

"That is true," our liege lord said. "At least, I have never heard of such a thing."

"Nor will you," the other man interrupted. "But those others, my lord! You know yourself that they are doing their utmost to obstruct the building of this bridge. And when they saw they were not succeeding, or in other words, when their despicable schemes were scotched by your lordship, they then produced the idea of destroying the bridge. First they placed their hopes in the fury of the river, but then, when nature did not help them, they sent their people to damage our bridge."

He paused again briefly, as if to let his audience take in what he said. It was clear, as I had suspected, that the water people would not give up the struggle easily. They were paying the road people back in their own coin. Apparently a battle over money was more savage than that fight between the crocodile and the tiger that the Dutchman had told me about.

"And that, my lord count, is in short the history of the matter."

Our count stared on imperturbably at the stooped delegate. At last, when the man had apparently had his say, he spoke:

"So what do you want of me, gentlemen?"

The leader of the delegation fixed his gaze on the count's eyes once again, as if to say, Do you really not understand what we want?

"We want the culprits punished," he said in a perfectly dry tone.

Our liege lord spread his arms. A bluish light filtered through the stained glass of the upper portion of the window, seeming to dissolve you and carry you far away. The count kept his arms open.

"It's no use asking that from me," he said finally. "I have never meddled in your business, and I have no intention of doing so now."

"And so shall we do the murder ourselves?"

"What?"

The pens of the scribes scratched disconsolately in the silence. The dim bluish light seemed to take your breath away.

"What?" said the leader of the delegation, hunched, almost fallen on the table.

The master-in-chief's red poll was opposite him, like a cold fire.

"You mentioned a murder," the count said.

Their eyes were again fixed on each other.

"A punishment," the visitor said.

"Ah yes, a punishment."

The silence continued after the scratching of the quills ceased, when any silence becomes unbearable.

Everybody expected the words of our liege lord to fill this lull. His voice came, weary and indifferent, as if from beyond the grave.

"If it is true, as you say, that your enemies have hit upon the idea of destroying the bridge with the help of legend, then you in turn could use the same means of punishing the culprits. . . . In other words . . ."

The count left the phrase unfinished, which happened extremely rarely.

The strangers' eyes burned feverishly.

"I understand, my lord count," their leader said at last.

He raised his body from the seat, although his back and head remained hunched over the table, as if they could not be detached from it. It was apparently not easy for him to move his back, and he remained thus for a very long time, while the others turned their heads toward the master-in-chief, almost as if he, who knew the secrets of bridges, could help to lift that arched backbone.

The man finally succeeded in standing up, and after bidding the count farewell, the delegation left one by one. I left too.

It was bad weather outside. The north wind froze my ears. As I walked, I could not stop thinking of what they had talked about with the count. Something ominous had been discussed in a mysterious way. Everything had been carefully shrouded. I had once seen the body of a mur-dered man on the main road, two hundred paces from the Inn of the Two Roberts. They had wrapped him in a cloth and left him there by the road. Nobody dared to lift the cloth to see the wounds. They must have been terrible.

The thought that I had involuntarily taken part in a conspiracy to murder disturbed my sleep all night. My head was heavy next morning. Outside, everything was dismal. Old, iron-heavy rain fell. Oh God, I said to myself, what is the matter with me? And a wild desire seized me to weep, to weep heavy, useless tears, like this rain.

29

T HE RAIN CONTINUED ALL THAT WEEK, as drearily as on that day of the discussion. People say that rain like this falls once in four years. The heavens seemed to be emptying the whole of their antiquity on the earth.

In spite of the bad weather, work on the bridge did not pause for a single day. Builders stopped abandoning the site. Work on the second and third arches proceeded at speed. Sometimes the mortar froze in the cold, and they were obliged to mix it with hot water. Sometimes they threw salt in the water.

The Ujana e Keqe swelled further and grew choppier, but did not mount another assault on the bridge. It flowed indifferently past it, as if nothing had happened, and indeed, to a foreign eye there was nothing but an ordinary bridge and river, like dozens of others that had long ago set aside the initial quarrels of living together and were now in agreement on everything. However, if you looked carefully, you would see that the Ujana e Keqe did not reflect the bridge. Or, if its furrows cleared and smoothed somewhat, it only gave a troubled reflection, almost as if what loomed above it were not a stone bridge but the fantasy or labor of an unquiet spirit.

Everyone was waiting to see what the spirits of the waters would do next. Water never forgets, old people said. Earth is more generous and forgets more quickly, but water never.

They said that the bridge was carefully guarded at night. The guards could not be seen anywhere, but no doubt they watched secretly among the timbers.

30

As soon as it had put its affairs in order, the deputation departed, leaving only one man behind. This was the quietest among them, a listless man with watery, colorless eyes. He kept to himself, as if not wanting to interfere in anyone's business, and he often walked quite alone by the riverbank. Mad Gjelosh — who knows why — imagined that he had a special right to threaten and insult this man whenever he saw him. The flaccid character noticed the idiot's wild behavior with surprise, and did his best to keep out of his way.

One day I happened to meet him face to face; he spoke to me first, apparently remembering me from the discussion with the count. We strolled a while together. He said that he was a collector of folktales and customs. I wanted to ask what this had to do with the bridge builders but suddenly changed my mind. Perhaps it was those watery eyes that made me think better of it.

A few days later he came to the presbytery, and we talked for a considerable length of time about Balkan tales and legends, some of which he knew. The tranquil water of his gaze became suddenly troubled whenever I mentioned them, despite his attempts to control his somnolent eyes.

"Ever since I have got to know them, I can't stop talking about them," he continued, as if trying to apologize.

I recollected in a flash the delegation's interest in legends, and also how our count had mentioned them during the discussion. Now I no longer had any doubt that I was really talking to a collector of legends. Nevertheless, deep down inside myself, something thudded, calling for my attention. It was a summons or a vision that fought to reach my brain but could not. I do not know what kind of fog prevented it.

"I hope I am not irritating you by saying the same things over and over again," he continued.

"On the contrary," I said. "It is a pleasure for me. Like most of the monks in these parts, I myself take an interest in these things."

As we walked along the sandbank, I explained to him that the legends and ballads of these parts mainly dealt with what had most distressed people throughout the ages, the division of mankind into the two great tribes of the living and the dead. The maps and flags of the world bear witness to dozens of states, kingdoms, languages, and peoples, but in fact there are only two peoples, who live in two kingdoms: this world, and the next. In contrast to the petty kingdoms and statelets of our world, these great kingdoms have never touched each other, and this lack of touch has pained most of all the people on this side. No testimony, no message, has so far ever come from the other side. The people on this side, unable to endure this rift, this absence of a crossing, have woven ballads against the barrier, imagining its destruction. Thus these ballads mention those in the next world, in other words the dead, crossing to this side temporarily with the permission of their kingdom, for a short time, usually for one day, to redeem a pledge they have left behind or to keep a promise they have made.

"Ah, I see," he said now and then, while his eyes stared as if begging me to continue.

I said that this is at least how we think on this side. In other words, we are sure that they make efforts to reach us, but that is only our own point of view. Perhaps they think differently, and if they heard our ballads they would split their sides laughing . . .

"Ah, you think that they probably do not want to come to us?"

"Nobody can know what they think," I replied. "Besides Him above."

A few black birds, those that they call winter sparrows, flew above us. He asked whether all the ballads sung were old, and I explained that sometimes new ones were devised — or rather, that is what people thought, whereas in fact all they did was revive forgotten ones.

I told him that an incident in the neighboring county ninety years ago, at the time of the first plague, had become the occasion for a new legend. A bride who had married into a distant house returned to her native land and, unable to explain her journey, declared that her dead brother had brought her home . . .

"Ah, it seems to me that I have heard it," he interrupted me. "A bride called Jorundina, if I am not mistaken."

"Jorundina or Doruntina. We pronounce it both ways."

"It is a heavenly ballad. Especially the suspicions against the young bride and her defense based on the promise her brother had made to her while he was alive. . . . There is a special word in your language . . ."

"*Besa,*" I said.

"*Baesa,*" he repeated with a grimace, as if he could not get his tongue around the word and could barely extract it from his mouth.

"For years on end there were investigations to shed light on the secret. All kinds of suspicions were raised, and all kinds of explanations were given, but later all these were forgotten and it remained a legend."

"Thank God," he said. "It would be a sin to lose such a pearl."

My pleasure that he appreciated the legend so much led me to say things that I would otherwise have avoided. I said, for instance, that whereas the Orthodox Church had several times tried to prohibit it, the ballad was now sung everywhere at Easter celebrations, and not only at feasts in Arberia, but throughout all the territories of the Balkans.

He listened to me, all eyes and ears.

"Because we fight over everything here on this peninsula, and not only over pastures and sheep, you can imagine that there have been quarrels even over the authorship of legends."

"Just think of that," he said.

"Even though everybody insists on claiming this legend for his own land, our monks think that it was born here. This is not because the event really happened in this country but because only among the Albanians has the *besa* become so charged with meaning."

"No doubt," he said. His eyes remained half closed, and it seemed that his mind was elsewhere. "Magnificent," he murmured. "The living and the dead trying to climb on the same cart . . . because, as we know, there is something dead in every living person, and vice versa."

He talked as if to himself, and meanwhile covered half his face with the collar of his cloak.

"I am keeping my left eye from the wind," he said to me, although I had not shown any sign of suspicion.

For part of the way, we spoke about other legends. They always concerned the prohibition against crossing from one world to the other and the temptation to transgress it. A man who tried to climb out of the pit of hell. Another who, having been transformed into a snake, attempted again to assume human form. A wall that demanded a sacrifice in order not to fall . . .

"A sacrifice?" he almost shrieked.

His brow darkened, and it was not just gloom but the opening of a chasm. He continued to hide half his face with his collar, but even what was visible was enough to make your flesh creep.

"A wall demanding a sacrifice . . . This is the legend of immurement, if I am not mistaken."

"It is, sir," I replied, quite coldly, I do not know why. "But you seem to know it."

"I know it. But I would like to hear it again. Tell it to me," he said in a lost voice, as if in a plea for help.

He now seemed far away, despite his attempts to smile. I could almost sense the reason for his anxiety. It was somewhere close to me. I could almost touch it. Ah, just a moment, I thought, just a moment. It will appear of its own accord.

"A wall that demanded a human being in a cavity . . . as it were, to acquire a soul . . . tell it to me," he said again. "And take no notice of me. I am like a child, and when I like something, I like to hear it a dozen, a hundred times in a row."

I began to tell him the legend of the castle of Shkodër, just as I had heard it years ago from my mother. There were three brothers, all masons, who were building the walls, but their work was not going well because what they built in the day was destroyed in the night.

Suddenly the reason for his distress came as clear to me as sunlight. You had to have the brains of Gjelosh not to grasp the similarity between the castle in the legend and the damaged bridge.

"What they built during the day was destroyed in the night," he murmured in a soporific voice, as if lulling himself to sleep.

I could not look him in the eye.

"What could they do?" I went on, involuntarily lowering my voice. "A wise old man told them that the wall collapsed because it demanded a sacrifice. And so they decided to immure one of their brides in the foundations."

"A sacrifice," he said, uselessly.

"Yes, a sacrifice," I whispered. "Since to immure someone means killing them."

"Killing them . . ."

"Of course. And they say that even if a person's shadow is walled up inside a bridge, that person must die, and then . . ."

90

"Yes, yes," he groaned.

"But which bride?" I continued. "They argued over the matter at great length and decided to sacrifice the bride who brought them their midday meal the next day."

"But," he interrupted. "But —"

"They gave their *besa* to each other that they would not tell their wives about the decision they had made. And so, as you see, we have the *besa* again. Or rather the *besa* and treachery woven together."

"Yes, *baesa*."

The word now seemed to stretch and tear at the corners of his mouth, and I would not have been surprised to see a trickle of blood.

I wanted to say that here, just as in the first tale, the motif of the *besa*, according to our monks, proves the Albanian authorship of the ballad. But there was some kind of . . . how shall I put it . . . fatal urgency in his expression that forced me too to talk fast.

"And that night two brothers, the oldest and the second, told their wives, and so broke the *besa*. The youngest brother kept it."

"Ah," he exclaimed.

"The two older brothers broke the *besa*," I repeated, hardly able to swallow my saliva.

This was exactly the right place to explain to him that these words "to break the *besa*" are, in the Slavic version of the ballad, *vjeru pogazio*, which mean "to violate faith" or "to outrage religion," and are quite meaningless in the Slavic version. This is because of an erroneous translation from the Albanian, mistaking the word *besa* for *besim*, meaning belief, religion. However, he would not let me pause. He had grasped my hand, and softly, very softly, as if asking me about a secret, he said, "And then?"

"Then morning came, and when their mother-in-law as usual tried to send one of the brides with food for the masons, the two older wives who knew the secret pretended to be sick. So the youngest set out, and they immured her, and that is all."

I raised my eyes to look at his face, and almost cried out. All the standing moisture of his old man's eyes had drained away, and those empty eyes now resembled the cavities in a statue. Like death, I thought. That is how her eyes must have looked.

31

THROUGHOUT THE FOLLOWING DAYS he was always seeking me out, and as soon as he found me he would do what he could to bring the conversation around to the immurement of the bride. He spoke of it as if it were an event that had happened two weeks before, and as if he was charged with its investigation. Gradually he involved me too. For hours on end I could think of nothing but a semidesert place under a scorching sun, where three workmen kept building walls that could never be finished. As we talked about the legend, we carefully analyzed it strand by strand, trying to account for its darker sides and to establish a logical link between its contradictory parts.

He asked me which of the three brides had children, and whether perhaps the youngest had none, as was easy to believe, and whether this was the reason why she was the one who was sacrificed. But I explained to him that all three had children, and I even apologized for not telling him the end of the story, in which the young wife who was immured begged her murderers (I used the actual word) to leave one breast outside the wall, so that even after her death she could suckle her child. He nearly lost his temper at my omission, shaking his finger almost threateningly at me, and told me not to do such a thing ever again. Because we were both of us at the time steeped in a strange world, his threat made no impression on me, although this is not something that I could normally forgive anyone. At this point I also told him about the curse that the sacrificed wife lays on the stonework in the two famous lines:

> *O tremble, wall of stone,*
> *As I tremble in this tomb!*

"This can be taken in a technical way," he butted in. "Because . . . at least bridges . . . every bridge in a way sways all the time."

This interjection on his part made no particular impression on me, but when a little later he said that immuring a person in fact weakens a structure, I interrupted:

"Tell me, please, whether you are a collector of tales or a builder."

"Oh," he said. "I'm in no way a builder, but I've learned something about the subject from working alongside builders. In fact, all great building works resemble crimes, and vice versa, crimes resemble . . ." He laughed. "For me, there is no difference between them. Whenever I find myself in front of columns I can clearly see blood spattering the marble, and the victim might replace a cathedral."

Whenever he left I felt dumbfounded.

One day he knocked before dawn to tell me something new that he had thought of during the night. I was still sleepy and could barely take in what he said. Finally I understood. He was saying that in his opinion the youngest brother too must have told his wife everything on that unforgettable night before the sacrifice.

"How is that possible?" I said. "How could a young woman then go to the masons knowing the fate that awaited her?"

"I knew you would say that," he said. "But I have thought of everything." He moved closer to me. "Listen to this. The youngest wife agreed to be sacrificed voluntarily, because her sisters-in-law and mother-in-law had made life hell for her."

"Hmm," I said. "Rather strange."

"There is nothing strange about it," he went on. "Between a daily hell and immurement, she chose the latter. Do you know what a quarrel among sisters-in-law means? Ah, I'm sorry, you're a monk."

"But what about him?" I asked. "What do you think about his attitude?"

"Whose?"

"Her husband's."

"I have thought long and hard about that too. No doubt he knew that she suffered but never imagined that matters could be so bad as to drive her to self-destruction. So the next day, when he saw his own wife arrive carrying the basket of food, his blood must have frozen. What do you think?"

"I don't know what to say," I replied. "Perhaps you are right, but perhaps it wasn't like that at all."

I was in fact certain that it had not been like that.

Whenever he came to see me, he had some new explanation. Once he told me that the youngest brother had perhaps not told his wife the secret, not out of a desire to keep the *besa* with his brothers but because he did not love his wife and had found a way to get rid of her. Another time he suggested that perhaps the three brothers had colluded among themselves to kill the youngest wife, and the whole fiction that the walls demanded a sacrifice was just a way of justifying the murder. All his interpretations of the legend were founded on baseness, betrayal, and disloyalty, and whenever he left I would be annoyed with myself for having listened to him. When he departed for the last time, he had sown the seed of doubt over not only the behavior of the three mason brothers and the two sisters-in-law but also that of the mother-in-law, who in his view certainly took part in the oath, and even that of the sacrificed bride herself. After he had left, after slinging mud at everything, not sparing even the dead, I decided I would tell him that he was free to think what he liked, but I had no desire to hear any more of his perverted speculations.

I waited for him the next day, to tell him that his efforts to throw mud at this old tragedy were useless, because the true kernel of the legend was the idea that all labor, and every major task, requires some kind of sacrifice, and that this magnificent idea is embodied in the mythologies of many peoples. What was new, and peculiar to the ballad of the Balkan peoples, was that the sacrifice was not connected with the outbreak of war or some march, nor even a religious rite, but concerned a wall, a work of construction. And this can perhaps be explained by the fact that the first inhabitants of these territories, the Pelasgians, were the first masons in the world, as the ancient Greek chronicles themselves admit.

I wanted to say that in truth the drops of blood in the legend were nothing but streams of sweat, but we know that sweat is a kind of humble nameless servant in comparison with blood, and therefore nobody has devoted songs and ballads to it. So it can be considered normal in a song to represent a river of sweat with a few drops of blood. It is of course obvious that alongside his sweat every man sacrifices something of himself, like the youngest brother, who sacrificed his own happiness.

I could hardly wait to tell him these and other ideas, but just when I had made up my mind to speak out, he disappeared. From that time on, I never saw him again.

32

I N SPITE OF THE SEVERE COLD, work on the bridge continued. It was said that they had now quite completed the second main arch and had begun the third. I say "it was said," because in fact nothing could be discerned from the bridge's external appearance behind its confusion of timbers!

Nothing worth recording occurred in the following weeks. The old blackened raft continued to pass from one bank to the other. The ferryman looked more hunchbacked than ever. The words "Boats and Rafts" on the rusty sign were barely legible. Two planks of the raft had broken loose, and no one bothered to repair them. Everything now quickly decayed, and the black water visible through the gaping planks of the raft seemed to make the expressions of its passengers even gloomier.

At dusk one Sunday (this is the only event that I can even partially remember), some people wearing black sheepskins crossed the river by raft, in somber haste. The fog seemed to swallow them as soon as they disembarked on the opposite bank. It was not long before some more people, also in black sheepskins, asked for the raft. They were just as gloomy and in as great a hurry as the first group. They asked about the men who had crossed before, and these were the only words to escape their lips as they crossed the river. One of them vomited continuously.

33

ONE MORNING, as I walked along the frozen river-bank in the hope of catching sight of the collector of tales and legends (for I did not know then that he had vanished forever), I came face to face with the master-in-chief. The north wind was piercing. Especially it had frozen his eyes, coating them with a kind of glittering film that prevented you from seeing what was inside them.

To my astonishment, this stern, gruff man greeted me. Only then did I realize how eager I was to get to know him. We exchanged a few words and set off walking side by side along the sandbank. The icy crust that coated his eyes seemed to crack in two or three places, making them even more inscrutable. I had imagined that talking with this man would be difficult, but not to this extent. Our conversation was a rambling, muddled affair, a real maze from which you could not extricate yourself. It was evident that he himself found it painful. It was apparently easier for him to construct bridges or towers than to conduct a human conversation. The worst of it was that I still sensed that something valuable, perhaps very valuable, lay at the bottom of this tangle, and it was precisely my efforts to understand this that upset me most. When I left him, my head felt cleft in two. I sat down by the fire and once more did my best to recollect the tangle. I began to unravel it carefully, thread by thread, and eventually I seemed to succeed. The essence of what he had said was this: According to signs that he had been studying for some time, the lineaments of a new order that would carry the world many centuries forward had faintly, ever so faintly, begun to appear in this part of Europe. These signs included the opening of new banks in Durrës, growing numbers of Jewish and Italian intermediaries dealing in twenty-seven different kinds of coin, and the almost universal acceptance of the Venetian ducat as a form of international currency. There was also the increasingly heavy traffic of merchant caravans, the organization of trade fairs, and especially (Oh Lord! How he emphasized that word "especially"), especially the construction of roads and stone bridges. And all this movement, he said, was a sign simultaneously of life and death, of the birth of a new world and the death of the old. He said something about bridges and the difficulties of building them, and during this part of the conversation I felt as if I were crushed under the rubble of a bridge that he had brought down upon me. But then he explained to me that, of all the monstrosities that deface the earth's surface, there never had been and never would be anything uglier than corpse-bridges. These bridges are born dead, he said, and they live in death (he used the phrase "they die all their lives") until the time comes for their demolition (or "ultimate death," as he put it). He told me that he had built such bridges himself and that now they appeared in his dreams like ghosts. If ever he decided to commit suicide (he told me), he would hang himself from such a bridge. I could scarcely understand what they were. They were not bridges built over rivers or streams or chasms, or indeed over any kind of gap that had to be crossed. They were bridges built in the middle of fields, and their only service was now and then to carry on their backs great ladies, who climbed on them to observe the sunset together with their invited guests. Building bridges was in fashion now, he said, and many princes and pashas considered them to be the same as the porches of their houses. I have built such phantoms, he said. He indicated with his hand the furrowed, foaming waters of the Ujana e Keqe, over which the stone bridge loomed, grim and unloved, and he added: "But this kind of bridge, even if washed in blood, is a thousand times nobler than those."

And that was more or less my conversation with him.

34

I N THE FIRST WEEK OF MARCH the bridge was damaged again. This time the damage was mainly below
the waterline and was extremely worrying. Large stone
blocks had been dislodged from the piers of the main
arch, and this, they said, would endanger the whole central portion of the bridge if repairs were not made at
once.

Suspended by ropes above the icy water, the workmen
attempted to fill the cavities. Besides being an exceptionally difficult task, this patchwork seemed in vain as long
as the stones were put in place without mortar. However,
if the repairs were postponed until summer, when the waters subsided and the use of mortar became possible,
there was a danger that the waters would further erode
the cavities.

As if bending over someone's wounds, new faces that
had come specially for this work swarmed all day over
the damaged places. It was said that they were trying a

new way of fixing stones with a mixture of wool, pitch, and egg-white.

The new damage to the bridge caused, as expected, a fresh storm of evil premonitions. People came from all over to see with their own eyes the cursed bridge, which had brought down on itself the wrath of the naiads and water spirits. That the damage was invisible made it even more frightening.

Together with the curious travelers, a horde of bards came, some returning in disappointment from an unfinished war somewhere among the principalities of the north, and others appearing here for the first time. These latter took their places at the Inn of the Two Roberts, and every night sang old ballads in eerie voices.

They told me that one of these ballads was that of the three mason brothers and the young wife immured in the castle that was built by day and destroyed at night. I remembered the collector of tales and customs, but I do not know what it was that impelled me to set off for the Inn of the Two Roberts to listen to the ballad with my own ears.

It was chilly, but nevertheless I set off on foot. Perhaps because of the potholes and puddles on the highway, I could not banish from my mind the watery eyes of the vanished collector of tales.

As soon as I heard the ballad's first verses, I recognized his hand in its composition. The ballad had been changed. It was not about three brothers building a castle wall, but about dozens of masons building a bridge. The bridge was built during the day and destroyed at night by the spirits of the water. It demanded a sacrifice. Let someone come who is willing to be sacrificed in the piers of the bridge, the bards sang. Let him be a sacrifice for the sake of the thousands and thousands of travelers who will cross that bridge winter and summer, in rain and storm, journeying toward their joy or to their misfortune, hordes of people down the centuries to come.

"Have you heard this new ballad that has appeared?" the innkeeper said to me. "The old one was better."

I did not know what to say. The bard sang on in a spine-chilling voice:

> *O tremble, bridge of stone,*
> *As I tremble in this tomb!*

"Yesterday I heard them say that every bridge does in fact tremble a little, all the time," the innkeeper went on.

I nodded. There flashed through my mind the thought that the collector of tales knew something about bridge building, perhaps as much as the master-in-chief.

I returned homeward in utter misery. From a distance the bridge stood blue in the falling dusk. Even if it were washed a thousand times in blood . . . the master-in-chief had said.

Clearly the ballad portended nothing but blood.

Along the entire road, I thought about the coming sacrifice. My head swam. Would he come to the bridge himself, like the youngest brother's wife, or would he be caught in a trap? Who would it be? What reason would he have to die, or to be killed? The old ballad entangled itself in my head with the new one, like two trees unsuccessfully trying to graft themselves onto each other. What would happen the evening before in the house of the man to be sacrificed? And what would be his reason for setting out to die, on a moonless night, as the old song put it?

Nobody will come, I suddenly said almost aloud. That collector of tales was just mad. But deep in my heart I felt afraid that someone would come. He would come slowly, with soft footsteps through the darkness, and lay his head on the sacrificial block. Who are you who will come? I asked myself. And why will you come?

35

S OME TRAVELERS who slept at the inn of the Two
Roberts brought disturbing news. It was said that the
Turks had finally succeeded in forcing Byzantium to cede
its part, in other words half, of the Vlorë base in a few
months' time. What they had sought from Aranit Komneni for so long in vain, they had managed to snatch from
the ailing empire. If this grim news was indeed true,
Aranit Komneni would from now on share the base as a
"partner" with the royal Turkish tiger. And it is well
known what life is like with a tiger in its lair.

The news shocked everybody, especially our liege
lord. People said that Aranit had sent letters to all the Albanian nobles and that a state of war had all but been declared in Vlorë.

36

THE MARCH DAYS rolled by like chunks of ice. Nobody could remember such a bitterly cold spring in years. The news about the Orikum base at Vlorë was true. The decision to hand over the Byzantine portion of the base to the Turkish Empire was proclaimed by special decree in the two imperial capitals, Constantinople and Brusa.

The news caused deep despair everywhere. It was said that the courts of Europe could not believe that ancient Byzantium could submit to such an indignity. Some made allowances, saying that this was at present the only way of staving off the Turkish monster. At present . . . But later?

News came from Vlorë of preparations for the evacuation of the Byzantine warships. Apparently the base would be vacated very soon. The Scandinavian garrison too was preparing to make way for the Turks.

The elderly prince of Vlorë kept his army mobilized.

They said that he himself was seriously ill but was keeping his illness secret.

As if these dark clouds were not enough, the bards at the Inn of the Two Roberts continued singing about the sacrifice that must be made at the bridge.

Work proceeded feverishly on the bridge. Ever since I had heard the most recent ballad, in which the immured victim cursed the bridge to perpetual trembling, it seemed to me that the bridge had really begun to shake.

37

For several consecutive days carts loaded with barrels of pitch passed along the western highway. The ferryman poled them across the river, cursing the wagoners, the pitch, and the entire world.

They said that the pitch was urgently needed at the Vlorë base. That is how it has always happened. As soon as tar begins to move fast along the highways, you know that blood will flow after it.

Meanwhile dire foreboding continually thickened around us, or, I would say, around everything that centered upon this cursed bridge. Now it was not merely the bards who went on casting their grim spell night and day at the Inn of the Two Roberts. No, this matter was now a topic of general conversation from morning to night; strangest of all, it became a most simple and natural thing to talk about a sacrifice, as if it were the weather or the crops. The idea of sacrifice, up to now a truth within a song, had emerged from its cocoon and suddenly crept up on us. Now it moved among us, alive and on equal terms with all the other concerns of the day.

On the roads, at home, and in taverns along the great highway, people talked of the reward the bridge and road builders would give to the family of the man who would allow himself to be sacrificed in the bridge piers. I could not accustom myself to this transition at all. Things that had been savage and frightening until yesterday had suddenly become tame. Everybody talked about the sum of money the immured man's family would receive, and people even said that, apart from the cash payment, they would receive for a long time to come a percentage of the profits from the bridge, like everyone else who had met its expenses. Other people gave even more astonishing explanations. They said that the compensation due to every member of the family had been worked out in the minutest detail, with every kind of eventuality borne in mind. Everything had been provided for, from the possibility of the victim being without relatives, an odd man out, as they say (which was difficult to believe), to the opposite case of a poor man who might have a wife, parents, and a dozen children. They had anticipated everything, from the possibility of an orphan (in which case, in the absence of heirs, the remaining portion of the reward would be spent on a chapel for his soul that would be built just next to the bridge piers) to the case of a needy man, who would be given a first and final chance of property to leave to his nearest and dearest, in just the same way as a meadow or a mill is left as a bequest, except that this property would be his death. They said that the planning had been so thorough that they had even provided for the sacrifice of rich men, in other words death for a whim, out of boredom with life, or simply for fame. In this case, if the immured victim did not care for the reward, the cash would be used to erect, besides the chapel, a statue or memorial, also next to the bridge piers.

They said that all these calculations had been put down on paper and fixed with a seal, so that anybody who was thinking of being immured could read them beforehand.

To me all this resembled a bizarre dream. This was something we had never heard of before, a kind of death with accounts, seals, and percentages. We were quite unused to it. Sometimes I could not take it in at all. I called to mind the delegation and its talks with the count, and what the collector of legends and the bridge's master-in-chief had said, and I tried to establish some connection between these things, but the more I brooded the more perplexed I became. This business of calculated sacrifice confused me completely.

Sometimes I told myself that perhaps these were the signs of the new order that the master-in-chief had told me about in that unforgettable conversation. That jumble of words had been full of contracts, accounts, currency exchange, and percentages, percentages, percentages on everything. Even on death.

38

IT WEIGHED ON ME like a fatal burden. Its stone piers crushed me. One of its arches planted itself directly on my stomach, another on my throat. I wanted to break free and save myself from it, but it was impossible. The only movement I could make was a slight, a very slight tremor. . . . Ah yes, I thought, this was the perpetual trembling of which the ballad spoke. A cry rose in my throat. The cry struggled to come out, pressing against the stone arch. This went on a long time. Then, I do not know how, something was released inside me, and I budged. In that same moment, with eyes closed in terror, I felt the bridge collapse and fall on my body.

I woke drenched in sweat. The room was stuffy. I rose to open the window. Outside a warm, damp wind blew. One could sense that the sky, though invisible, was overcast. Some silent flashes of lightning burst against the mute flatness.

"Oh Lord," I cried aloud, and I lay down again on my bed. But further sleep eluded me. A few awkward ideas, with a deceptive glitter as if frozen by winter, floated somewhere inside me. I do not know how long I remained in this state. When I finally opened my eyes, it was light. Somebody was knocking at the outside door. There was an anxious rattle at the iron doorlatch. The sky was cloudy, but not as overcast as I had imagined. Spring has unexpectedly come, full of fury, I said to myself.

Two village neighbors were at the door, with distraught faces. Their eyes were troubled and bloodshot.

"What is it?" I asked. "What's the matter?"

They raised their hands to their throats, as if trying to force out the words.

"At the bridge, Gjon ... Under the first arch ... They've walled up Murrash Zenebisha."

"No."

I was unable to say anything else, or even to think. But these people, who seemed to have lost the power of thought before me, expected something from me. Soon I found myself walking toward the bridge. We hardly walked but were blown where the wind bore us, like three waving scraps of rag, myself in the middle and the others on either side.

I knew Murrash Zenebisha. Among ordinary people, it would have been difficult to find anyone more commonplace than he. His appearance, his average height, and his whole life were ordinary to the point of weariness. I could not take in the fact that this extraordinary thing, immurement, had happened to none other than him. The more I thought about it, the more it seemed an aberration. It was more than turning into a leader or a statue. . . . Everything had gone too far . . . now he was divided from us by the mortar of legend.

From a distance, you could see a small gathering of people around the bridge pier. By the first arch. He must be there.

As I drew closer, I tried, I do not know why, to recall Murrash Zenebisha's commonplace face. Oh Lord, from this moment I could not picture it in my mind at all. It swam as if under a film of water, with a broken, uncanny smile.

The small group of people moved silently to make room for me. Nobody greeted me. They stood like candles, looking strangely small against the background of the bridge. A part of the arch bent heavy and chill above them.

"There he is," a quiet voice said to me.

He was there, white like a mask, spattered with plaster, only his head and neck, and part of his chest. The remainder of his trunk, and his arms and legs, were merged with the wall.

I could not tear my eyes from him. There were traces of fresh mortar everywhere. The wall had been strengthened to contain the sacrifice. (A body walled up in the piers of a bridge weakens the structure, the collector of tales had said.) The bulging wall looked as if it were pregnant. Worse, it looked as if it were in birth pangs.

The body seemed planted in the stone. His stomach and legs and the main portion of his trunk were rooted deep, and only a small portion of him emerged.

A wall that demands a human being in its cavity, the collector of customs had said. Foul, sinful visions taunted me. The wall indeed looked pregnant. . . . But this was a perverse pregnancy. . . . No baby emerged from it, on the contrary, a human being was swallowed up. . . . It was worse than perverse. It would have been perverse if, in contrast to a baby who emerges into the light, the man who entered the darkness were to shrink and be reduced to the size of an infant and then to nothing. . . . But that was not to happen. This was a perversion of everything. It was perversity itself.

Around me, people's voices came as if from the next world.

"When?" asked the hushed voice of a new arrival.

"Just after midnight."

"Did he feel much pain?"

"None at all."

I heard sobbing close beside me. Then I saw his wife. Her face was swollen with tears, and in her arms she carried a year-old baby, who was trying to nuzzle her breast. Paying no attention to the men standing around, she had uncovered one breast. The breast was swollen with milk, and the nipple occasionally escaped from the baby's mouth. Her tears fell on her large white breast, and when the nipple missed the child's mouth, her tears mixed with drops of milk.

"He was very calm," explained one of the count's scribes, who had apparently come in search of explanations. "He asked about the terms of the agreement one more time, and then . . ."

A workman who stood holding a pail near the place of sacrifice splashed the dead man with wet plaster. The plaster trickled down the hair sticking to his brow, gave a sudden gleam to his open eyes, which was quickly quenched, and then patchily smeared his features before coursing down his neck and disappearing into the wall.

"Why are you throwing on plaster?" a nervous voice asked. But no one replied.

It seemed that they were sprinkling him at intervals, because after emptying its contents over the sacrifice, the worker went to refill his bucket from a nearby barrel.

His wife's interrupted sobbing became louder after the sprinkling.

"He didn't tell anyone about what he was going to do?" someone asked his wife softly.

She shook her head.

"No one," she said.

Only then did I notice the other members of the family, standing around his wife. His parents and two brothers with their wives were there. Their faces were petrified, as if they too had been splashed with that plaster of eternity.

"No one," his wife repeated. But I could not look at her eyes any longer, they were so swollen with weeping.

The count's scribe asked something of her too, and she gave a short answer. Then she turned to me and said something, but my eyes were fixed on the immured man; I stared at the lower part of his neck, at his collarbone, just where the cavity above his chest . . .

But at that moment the man standing by with the pail of plaster in his hands splashed him again, and once more the plaster ran down his forehead, igniting and at once quenching his vacant, blind, oblivious white eyes. Then the trickle meandered down his neck, quickly whitening the very spot from which I could not tear my eyes.

The baby had again missed his mother's nipple, and was whimpering. I asked the woman whether they had been in financial straits.

"No," she said. "He'd been earning plenty recently."

Recently, I thought. Like many inhabitants of the surrounding district, he had been working as a day laborer on the bridge and must have been receiving a normal wage, as normal as everything else in his life.

Another of the count's men arrived and whispered the same questions.

"When?"

"Just after midnight."

It seemed that we would all stand rooted to the spot, and people would arrive and mutter the same questions until the end of the world.

Now and again one could hear the words "brother, brother" from his sister. But his mother's sobbing was more muffled. Only once she said, "They killed you, son." And a little later she very softly added, "As if your mother had no need of you."

I would never have dared to interrupt a mother's lament, but the words "They killed you, son" gave me no peace.

"Is it possible someone killed him?" I said to her in a low voice. "But why?"

She wiped her tears.

"Why? How should a poor old woman like me know? No doubt for nothing. Because he cast a shadow on this earth."

"He had always been worried recently," said his wife by my shoulder. "He had something on his mind."

"And last night?"

"Last night particularly."

My eyes froze again on the dead man's neck just above the collarbone, as if something were about to appear there, a shadow, a . . . I do not know what to say. But the plasterer with his usual gesture once more emptied his pail of plaster over the immured man. The grayish white liquid, the very stuff of legend, poured over him.

"Last night particularly," his wife went on. "I thought I saw him move at midnight and get up. At dawn he was gone."

The milk from her breast had again missed her baby and trickled to the ground, but she seemed not to care.

"Did you need money?" someone asked.

"What can I say?" his wife asked. "Like everyone else."

The members of the dead man's family still stood grouped in silence. There was the splashing of the pail again as it was refilled with plaster from the barrel. I was completely numbed. I would not have been surprised if the man with the bucket had now coated us all with plaster.

39

ALL THAT DAY AND THE NEXT I was not at all myself. His open eyes fixed under their film of plaster seemed to stare from every wall around me. Walls terrified me, and I tried at all costs not to look at them. But they were almost impossible to avoid. I only then understood what an important and powerful part walls play in our lives. There is no getting away from them, like conscience. I could leave the presbytery building, but even outside there were walls, close by or in the distance.

My head was splitting in two with speculation. If he had really set out to sacrifice himself of his own free will, as everybody now claimed, what must his motive have been? The desire to ensure a better life for his wife and family, with the help of the great sum of money that the road firm would pay for the sacrifice? I could have believed this suspicion of many people, but not the modest Murrash Zenebisha. Sometimes I wondered whether he had gone to die in order to put an end to a family quarrel (you don't know what a quarrel among sisters-in-law is like), but this too was unbelievable. There had never been the least rumor of such a thing in the Zenebisha family. I sometimes asked myself whether, whatever his reasons for sacrificing himself, he had told his wife what was in his mind. And had she accepted his plan? It was impossible to believe such a thing. And then I wondered whether he perhaps did not love his wife. She had said that he sometimes went away at night, she did not know where. She had even begun to grow suspicious.

I knew myself that this was the kind of conjecture that, although I despised, I had nevertheless acquired from that collector of customs. I strove to free myself from it, as from the walls, but I could not.

Sometimes he would go away at night. . . . Was his wife really telling the truth? Were the others telling the truth? I too could have believed what was said, but that place in the victim's neck, there between his neck and collarbone, controverted everything. I had stared at it three times, because each time it had struck me that a spot under the layer of plaster had begun to blush faintly, very faintly, like a stain. But all three times the man with the pail had splashed plaster on the corpse before I could really detect a redness.

Enough, I thought. We have had nothing but babble and lies. We were dealing with a pure and simple crime. They had murdered Murrash Zenebisha. His mother had been the first to say the word: "They killed him for nothing. . . . Because he cast a shadow on this earth. . . ." They had murdered him in cold blood shortly after midnight and then walled him up. The wound, or one of his wounds, was between the neck and the collarbone, and the man with the pail had splashed plaster over him again and again to hide the possible bloodstain. It was a murder done by the road builders.

But how had Murrash Zenebisha come to be by the bridge at night? I asked this question out loud, because I had the satisfaction of being able to supply a clear answer. Sometimes he would go away at night. . . . And so shall we do the murder ourselves? . . . The road builders had let slip these words at the meeting with the count. Murrash Zenebisha's fate had been sealed on that day. And the count, withdrawing to one side, had done nothing but wash his hands like Pontius Pilate. The road builders had understood that the water people had instructed someone to damage the bridge at night. This person was the ordinary Murrash Zenebisha. He had done his job three times in a row. . . . The fourth time they had caught and killed him. He had been very worried recently. He had something on his mind. . . . And last night? Last night particularly. Everywhere bards were singing about his death. There was only one possibility left to him: to give up this job. However, "Boats and Rafts" would apparently not allow the agreement to be broken. After catching him in their trap, they would not let him back out. So there was nothing for him to do but become an outlaw, or continue on his fatal path. Apparently he had chosen the second. . . . He had something on his mind. And last night? Last night particularly. Possibly this was to have been his last task for the water people. He set out as on the other occasions shortly after midnight. He dived into the water a long way from the bridge and swam up to it, trying not to make any noise. The night was dark and moonless. What happened next at the bridge, no one would ever know. Perhaps they caught him on the spot, dislodging the stones, or in the water, trying to escape; no one knew. No one knew how they had killed him. They may have killed him at once, or perhaps they interrogated him for a time, and threatened him. Or they may have talked to him sweetly and reassuringly, reminding him of the lavish compensation his wife would receive. Or perhaps there had been neither threats nor sweet words, and they killed him in silence, everything done without words, in dumb show, under the arch of the bridge. Because this was only the final act of a murder that had been in the wind for a long time. Its spurts of blood had already spattered us all, and its screams had died away long ago.

The long duel between the men of the water and the men of the land had concluded with the victory of the latter. Do not try to harm us again, or you will be killed. That was the cry that came from the first arch of the bridge.

I was convinced of the truth of all this. But my mind was not entirely settled, and I continued silently to mull over innumerable theories.

If this was really what had happened, then the question followed of whether Murrash Zenebisha's wife was aware that he had agreed with "Boats and Rafts" to damage the bridge. And if she did know, what had her attitude been? But the initial question cropped up again before this. What had led Murrash Zenebisha into this danger? Desire for money? He was earning plenty. Besides, his brothers were masons like himself.

All this made my head swim. I felt that I had wandered into a maze of arguments from which I would never emerge. I returned to where I had started and circled around the same point: had his wife encouraged him in this affair or, on the contrary, held him back? Either was possible. Perhaps she had dreamed of a better life, of dressing better than her sisters-in-law, of finery. But it was also possible that she had said to her husband, Why do we need this damned money? Thank God, we don't live badly. Sometimes he would go away at night. . . . And she had even several times become suspicious. But what if he really wanted more money for another woman? He would go away at night. . . . There could be two reasons for his disappearing at night. First, to damage the bridge, and second, another woman. Or perhaps both together. Another woman, rather than his daily existence, was more likely to lead him to risk his life. His wife had become suspicious. Perhaps she had spied on him. He could have explained his absences by telling her about damaging the bridge (if he had indeed told her his secret). But even so, perhaps his wife had begun not to trust him. So she might have followed him on one of those nights, and when she discovered that he had a secret besides the bridge, she may in her subsequent fury (or, who knows? quite calmly) have informed the builders.

But in whatever way the incident had happened, its essence remained unchanged: the bridge builders had murdered Murrash Zenebisha in cold blood and immured him. The crime had only one purpose — to inspire terror.

They had calculated everything in advance. No doubt they had carried out detailed studies of all possible ways of justifying the crime. At the very beginning, before the bridge existed or was even sketched, they had started by sending a man who pretended to be seized by an epileptic fit on the very bank of the Ujana e Keqe. Not a bridge, not a sketch, but a sickness lay at the root of it all. That was the first blow. It was natural that death should follow.

Both sides, "Boats and Rafts" and the road company, used ancient legend in their savage contest. The former used it to stir up the idea of destroying the bridge, and the latter to plot a murder.

My exhausted brain contained an idea as dismal as it was wearyingly plain. I thought that, like all the affairs of this world, this story was both simpler and more involved than it appeared. . . . They had come from far away. One side came from the water, and the other from the steppes, to accomplish before our eyes something that, as their collector of customs said, could still not be understood for what it was: a bridge or a crime. For it was still unknown which of the two would survive longer on this earth and which would be eroded by the seasons. Only then would we understand which was the real edifice and which the mere scaffolding that helped in its construction, the pretext that justified it.

At first sight, it seemed that the newcomers had calculated everything, but perhaps that too was only a superficial view. Perhaps they themselves imagined they were building a bridge, but in fact, as if in delirium, they had obeyed another order, themselves not understanding whence it came. And all of us, as fickle as they, watched it all and were unable to discern what was in front of us: stone arches, plaster, or blood.

Holy Blessed Mary, forgive me these sins, I prayed silently. I succeeded in calming my soul, but my brain would not rest. It raced to the legends. These people had revived legend like an old weapon, discovered accidentally, to wound each other badly. It was nevertheless early to say whether they had really enlisted it in their service. Perhaps it was legend itself that had caught them in a snare, had clouded their minds, and had thrust them into the bloody game.

40

D URING ALL THOSE DAYS nobody talked of anything but the immurement of Murrash Zenebisha. People told the most incredible stories about what he supposedly said at the moment when they walled him in, and his last wish for a space to be left for his eyes so that he could see his year-old child. Some substituted the bridge itself for the child, and some tied his last wish not only to his family but to their duty, to the gods, and to the entire principality.

There was a constant crowd of people by the arch of the bridge where the victim was immured. The guards placed by the count watched over the body from morning to night, and there came a moment when the investigators assigned to probe the incident, after making their inquiries, themselves stood petrified in front of the dead man. His face, that white plaster mask, had undergone no change in the last few days. Now that the plaster was dry and they were no longer coating him, the whiteness of that face was unchanging. They said that if you looked at it by moonlight, you could lose your speech.

His family — his elderly parents, his brothers and their wives, and his young widow with the baby whose mother's nipple always missed his mouth — came every day and stood stock-still for whole hours, never taking their eyes off the victim. His open eyes with their crust of plaster had the silence and unresponsiveness of that "never ever" that only death can bring. During the first week his parents aged by a century, and the features of his brothers and their wives and even their infants seemed furrowed for life. But he, leaning against the arch of the bridge as if against a stone pillow, entirely smoothed over, studied them all beyond the plaster barrier that made him more remote than a spirit.

Whenever the crowd thinned or dispersed, mad Gjelosh would arrive at the site of the sacrifice. He was quite stunned by the scene, and his inability to understand what had happened mortified him considerably. He would walk slowly up to the body, approaching it sidelong, and softly whisper, "Murrash, Murrash," in the hope of making the man hear. He would repeat this many times and then disconsolately depart.

Old Ajkuna came on the seventh day, the day when it is believed that the dead make their first and most despairing attempt to break the shackles of the next world. She stayed for hours on end by the first arch, without uttering a word. That was something that could find no parallel in the experience of even the most elderly. A few more days passed, and then whole weeks, and the fortieth day was approaching, the day on which it was believed that a dead man's eyeballs burst, and then everybody realized what a great burden an unburied man was, not only on his family but on the entire district. It was something that violated everything we knew about the borders between life and death. The man remained poised between the two like a bridge, without moving in one direction or the other. This man had sunk into nonexistence, leaving his shape behind him, like a forgotten garment.

People came from all parts to see the unburied body: the curious from distant villages, and wayfarers who lodged at the inns on the great highway; even rich foreigners came, as they traveled idly to see the world together with their ladies. (Such a thing had come into fashion recently, after the dramatic improvements to the highway.)

They stood in awe by the first arch, noisy, waxenfaced, talking in their own languages and gesticulating. You could not tell from their gestures whether they blessed or cursed the hour that brought them to the bridge. Beyond all their hubbub, solitary, cold, vacant, aloof, and covered with lime, Murrash Zenebisha seemed to stand in silence like a bride.

It was the beginning of April. The weather was fine, and work proceeded on the bridge more busily than ever before. The dead man seemed to spur the work forward. The second span was now completely finished, and the vault of the third was being raised. Last year's filthy mud, which had dirtied everything round about, had gone. Now only a fine dust of noble whiteness fell from the carved stones and spread in all directions. It coated the two banks of the Ujana, and sometimes on nights of the full moon it shone and glittered in the distance.

On one of these moonlit April evenings I ran into the master-in-chief on the riverbank, quite by accident. I had not seen him for a long time. He seemed not to want to look me in the eye. The words we exchanged were quite meaningless and empty, like feathers that float randomly, lacking weight and reason. As we talked in our desultory way, I suddenly felt a crazy desire to seize him by the collar of his cape, pin him against the bridge pier, and shout in his face: "That new world you told me about the other day, that new order with its banks and percentages, which is going to carry the world a thousand years forward, it is founded on blood too."

In my mind I said all this to him, and even expected his reply: "Like all sorts of order, monk." Meanwhile, as if he had sensed my inner outburst, he raised his head and for the first time looked me in the eye. They were the same eyes that I now knew well, with rays and cracks, but inflamed, as if about to burst, almost as if it was the fortieth day not for the dead man at the bridge but for himself. . . .

41

S PRING WAS EXCEPTIONALLY CLEAR. The Ujana e Keqe brimmed with melted snow. Though full and renewed, the river mounted no attack on the bridge. It seemed not to notice it anymore. It foamed and roared around the stone piers and under the feet of the dead, but as it flowed on it spread out again, as if pacified by the sight of the victim. A wicked, mocking glint remained only in the cold crests of the waves.

All spring and at the beginning of summer, work continued busily. The third arch was almost finished, and work began on the right-hand approach arch.

Throughout its length the bridge echoed to the sounds of masons' hammers, chisels, picks, and the creaking of the carts. Amid the constant din of the building work and the roaring of the river, Murrash Zenebisha stood, coated as ever with plaster, solitary, white, and alien. Whether the flesh of his face had decayed under his plaster mask, or whether it had hardened like mortar, nobody could tell.

His family came as always, but gradually reduced the

length of their visits. Some days after his immurement, stunned by everything that had happened, they remembered that they had not even managed to weep for him according to custom. They tried to do so later, but it was impossible. Their laments stuck in their throats, and the words that should have accompanied their weeping somehow would not come. Then they tried hiring professional mourners, but these women too, although practiced in weeping under all kinds of circumstances, could not mourn, try as they might. He does not want to be wept for, his parents said.

Some time had passed since his death, and at times it seemed a source of joy to his family that they would have his living form in front of their eyes, but sometimes this seemed the worst curse of all. Now they no longer came together. His wife would come alone with her baby in her arms and, when she saw the others approaching, would leave. People said that they had quietly begun to quarrel over sharing the compensation.

The investigators also came less frequently. It seems that the count had other worries and would have liked to close the inquiry. However, this did not prevent the fame of Murrash Zenebisha from spreading farther every day. It was said that he had become the conversational topic of the day in large towns, and that the grand ladies of Durrës asked each other about him, as about the other novelties of the season.

Many people set off from distant parts with the sole object of seeing him. Sometimes they came with their wives, or even made the journey a second time. This was no doubt why the Inn of the Two Roberts had recently doubled its business.

42

THE WEATHER DETERIORATED. The count, together with his family, returned from the mountain lodge where he had spent the summer. At the bridge, the left-hand approach arch was being finished.

One day at the beginning of September the count's daughter came to see the immured victim. I had not seen her for some time. She had grown and was now a fine girl. I thought she would not be able to bear the sight of the dead man, but she endured it. As she left the sandbank, thin and somewhat woebegone, people turned their heads after her. They knew that the powerful Turkish pasha, whom ill fortune had recently made our neighbor, had quarreled with our liege lord because of this dainty girl.

Perhaps because she had spent her girlhood in such troubled times as recent seasons had been, no tales had been woven around her, such as those about knights crossing seven mountain ranges to meet a girl in secret, and the like, which are usually told about young countesses and the daughters of nobles in general. In place of such tales of love, there was only an alarming sobriquet attached to her, which, I do not know why, spread everywhere. They called her "the Turk's bride." I often racked my brains to explain such an irrational nickname. It was quite meaningless, because nothing like that had happened. It was the opposite of the truth, but the nickname clung to her. It could not conceivably have been created out of goodwill, or even malice, and so perhaps resembled a truth and a lie at the same time. The girl did not go to the Turks as a bride, but the nickname remained, as if it were unimportant whether the wedding took place or not, and the main thing was the proposal and not its acceptance. And so she was called "the Turk's bride" simply because the Turks had asked for her, had cast their eyes this far, and had brandished from a distance that black veil with which they cover their women.

The nickname made my flesh creep. Why was it still used, and why did it not perish the moment the Turk's proposal was rejected? What was this perpetual danger, this offer of marriage, that still floated on the wind? Sometimes I told myself that it was a chance nickname, more ridiculous than alarming, and not worth becoming upset about, but it was not long before my suspicions were aroused again. Did it all not extend beyond the fate of the noble young lady? Did popular imagination in some obscure, utterly vague way perhaps foresee a generally evil destiny for the girls of Arberia? This horrible nickname could not have arisen for nothing, still less have stuck to her like a burr.

I said these things to myself, and thought: If only that young girl knew what I was thinking as she walks along the bank with her nurse, her slight figure almost translucent!

43

HASTE WAS EVIDENT EVERYWHERE: in the works on the Ujana, in the pace of the heralds, and even in the flight of the storks, which, having pecked at the beams of the bridge for the last time, set off on their distant migrations that no rivers or bridges obstructed.

Even the news coming from the Orikum base was gathered in haste and was contradictory. It was said that the aged Komneni was dead but that his death was being kept secret because of the situation at Orikum. All kinds of other things were whispered. It was said that the great Turkish sultan had withdrawn into the interior of Asia to meditate in complete solitude about the general affairs of the world, and that this was the reason why the Turks seemed to have fallen asleep.

There was no sign of them. But one day, at the end of the week, another dervish was seen, wandering across the cold plain, a solitary figure amid the winds. Like all itinerant dervishes, he was barefoot and dust-covered, and perhaps for this reason seemed to have ash-colored rags instead of hair, and hair instead of rags. He paused at the first arch of the bridge, fell on his face in front of the victim, and intoned an Islamic prayer in a deep and mournful voice. Then he disappeared again, I do not know where, across the open plain.

44

A FEW DAYS before the final work on the bridge, one of the master-in-chief's two assistants, the fat one, fell ill with a rare and frightening disease: all the hairs on his body fell out. They shut him in a hut and tried in every possible way to keep his sickness secret, but there was no way it could be concealed. People gossiped about it all day, some with pity, some with fear, but most with mockery. Wolves molt in summer, they said, just like him. Mad Gjelosh wandered all day around the hut, putting his eye to cracks in the wall to see what he could. Then he emerged from the other side, nodding his head as if in understanding. Old Ajkuna said that this was only the beginning of God's punishment. Everybody who has taken part in this cursed business will lose first his hair, she said, then his eyes, nose, and ears, and in the end the flesh will fall from his bones piece by piece.

Meanwhile the workmen, always in haste, scrambled day and night among the mesh of scaffolding, scurrying everywhere like beetles, with pails, whetstones, and stone slabs in their hands. It seemed that they were cladding the sides because, in contrast to the stones of the piers and arches, this was soft limestone, easy to smooth and therefore called female stone. It was said that in some buildings in which it had been used long ago it oozed a white juice resembling milk, as if it were a woman's breast.

45

A T DAWN ON THE MORNING of the first Sunday of the
month of St. Dimiter, the bridge over the Ujana e
Keqe, which had in these two years brought us more
troubles than the river itself had brought stones and tree
stumps, stood complete.

Everyone knew that it was almost finished, but its appearance on that morning was quite amazing. This was
because the day before much of it had still been half hidden behind the confusion of planks, and they had only
begun removing the scaffolding, as if peeling the husk
from a corn cob, just before dusk. They had perhaps
planned it this way, so that at the dawn of day it would
stand clear, as if emerging from the womb of the gorge.

The hammers had echoed all night, dislodging the
wooden wedges that fell crashing down. In their sleep,
people thought they heard thunderclaps, turned heavily
in their beds, and cursed or were afraid. There were many
who thought that the laborers, repenting or following an

order from who knows where, were demolishing what they had built.

In the morning they were right not to believe their eyes. Under the clumsy light of day, between the turbid waters and the gloomy sky, it soared powerfully from one bank, sudden, dazzling, like a voicelike scream, and hung in suspense directly over the watery gulf as if about to launch itself in flight. But as soon as it reached midway over the river, its trajectory fell, like a dream of flying, and it gently bent its back until its span touched the opposite bank and froze there. It was lovely as a vision. The veins of the stone seemed both to absorb and emit light, like the pores of a living body. Thrust between the enmity of water and earth, it now seemed to be striving to strike some accord between the separate elements of its surroundings. The frothing wave crests seemed to soften toward it, as did the wild pomegranate bushes on the opposite hill, and two small clouds on the horizon.

They all strove to make room for it in their midst. Here is its shape: Three arches ⋒⋒⋒ and the cross † that marked the place of sacrifice.

People stood in awe on both sides of the Ujana and gaped at it openmouthed, as if it were a thing of wicked beauty. Nevertheless nobody cursed it. Not even old Ajkuna, who came at midday, could curse it. The stone has taken my mouth away, she seemed to say as she departed. In their total absorption in the spectacle, nobody paid the least attention to the throng of laborers preparing to leave. It was incredible that this mass of men and equipment, this pig run, this gang of vagrants that had tried the patience of wood and stone, this filth, this pack

139

of stammerers, liars, boozers, hunchbacks, baldheads, and murderers, could have given birth to this miracle in stone.

On one side, as if feeling themselves that they had suddenly become alien to their own creation, they gathered their paraphernalia, tools, mortar buckets, hammers, ropes, and criminals' knives. They heaved them helter-skelter onto carts and mules, and as I watched them scurrying about for the last time, I felt impatient, wanting them to leave. I wanted to be rid of them as soon as possible, and never hear of them again.

46

T HE LAST CONTINGENT of workmen left three days
later. They loaded on carts the heavy tools, great
mortar barrels, and all kinds of scrap iron and wheels
that creaked endlessly. They lifted the architect's sick assistant onto a covered cart, hiding him from people's
view, because they said that his appearance was not for
human eyes.

The deserted sandbank resembled a ruin, an eyesore
with half-destroyed sheds stripped of everything of value,
fragments of plank thrown anywhere, traces of mortar,
piles of shattered stones, carelessly discarded broken
tools, ditches, and lime pits half filled with water. The
right bank of the Ujana looked disfigured forever.

Before he boarded his cart, the master-in-chief, who
seemed to notice that I was watching their departure, left
his people and came up to me, apparently to bid farewell.
He said nothing but merely drew a piece of card from his
jacket. Scribbling some figures on it with a bit of lead, he
began to explain to me, I do not know why, the balancing

forces that held the bridge upright. My eyes opened wide, because I had not the slightest knowledge of such things, while he went on in his broken language, thinking that he was explaining to me what the forces and opposing forces were.

Late that afternoon the last cart left, and a frightening silence descended. I still had in my hand the draftsman's card, covered with lines and figures, which perhaps did show the forces that kept the bridge upright and those trying to bring it down. The setting sun gleamed obliquely on the arches, which at last found a broken reflection in the waters, and at that moment the bridge resembled a meaningless dream, dreamed by the river and both riverbanks together. So alien, dropped by the riverbanks into time, it looked totally solitary as it gripped in its stone limbs its only prey, Murrash Zenebisha, the man who died to allay the enmity of land and water.

47

W HAT WAS THIS? They had gone, and an unendurable silence reigned everywhere. A horrible calm. Almost as if plague had struck.

No one crossed the bridge. Not even mad Gjelosh. Chill winds blew upon it, passing in and out of its arches. And then the winds dropped, and the bridge hung in air, a stranger, superfluous. Human travelers who should have headed for it avoided the place, turning aside, back, or away, looking for the ford, calling softly to the ferryman; they were ready to swim across the river or freeze in its rapids and drown rather than set foot on the bridge. Nobody wanted to walk over the dead.

And so the first week passed and the second began. The great mass of stone waited expectantly. The empty arches seemed about to eat you. The bowed spine above waited for someone to step on it, no matter who — vagrants, women, a barbarian horde, wedding guests, or an imperial army marching two, four, twenty-four, one hundred hours without rest.

But nobody set foot on it. Sometimes it made you want to cry out: Had so much sweat, so much effort, and even . . . blood been expended for this bridge, never to be used for anything?

Rain fell the second week. For days on end the bridge stood drenched and miserable.

Then the rain stopped, and again the weather was chill and gray. The third week began. A whining wind crawled over the wasteland. It was the end of Tuesday afternoon when they saw that a wolf had padded softly over the bridge, as in a fairy tale. People could not credit their own eyes (and there were those who were ready to believe that a herald had crossed, waving the standard of the Skuraj family, the only one that has a wolf in its center). The beast meanwhile vanished quickly into the distance, where the wind seemed to have stood still, and howled.

The days that followed were silent and empty. It was ashen weather everywhere, as if before the end of the world. One afternoon, old Ajkuna came up to the bridge. People thought that finally she would curse it, and they gathered to watch. She halted at the entrance to the bridge, below the right-hand approach arch, and laid her hand and then her ear to the masonry. She stood there a long while, then lifted her head from the palm of her hand and said:

"It is trembling."

I remembered the man who had fallen in an epileptic fit. He had indeed passed on his convulsions to the bridge.

Many believed that the bridge would collapse of itself. Occasionally I brought out the card on which the designer had scribbled those mysterious figures, and I would study them abstractedly, as if trying to understand from them the bridge's fear.

I would have wished that the designer could have seen this desolation.

But the bridge's solitude, which seemed ready to last for centuries, came to an end suddenly one Sunday. The highway, the surrounding plain, and the sandbank echoed to a piercing creak. People ran in terror to see what was happening. On the ancient road, in a long black column like a crawling iron reptile, a convoy of carts was traveling. The carts approached the bridge. We all stood frozen on the bank, expecting to witness some catastrophe. The first cart quickened its speed and began to mount the incline. You could hear the iron wheels changing their tone as they struck the stone paving. Then the cart mounted the right-hand approach arch, and then on, on, over the first arch, over . . . the dead man. Then came the second and third carts, and then the others, all laden with blackened barrels. They squeaked frighteningly, especially when they rode over the immured victim, and it looked each time as if the arch would split, but nothing happened.

The tail of the convoy was still on the bridge when people realized what kind of caravan it was, what it carried, and where it was going. Its sole cargo was pitch, for the Orikum military base near Vlorë.

We watched its progress for a long time, looking alternately at the tail of the convoy and at the bridge, which had suffered no harm at all.

Immediately after the crossing of this inauspicious tar train, as a guest at the Inn of the Two Roberts called it, news came that the death of Komneni had at last been announced at Vlorë, and that his son-in-law, Balsha II, had deployed his troops over the entire principality, including Komneni's half of Orikum. Our count, accompanied by his entourage, departed to attend the old prince's burial. He must have been still on the road when, like thunder after a lightning flash, more news came, worse than the first, to tell us that the Byzantine garrison had finally evacuated its half of the naval base, ceding it to the Turkish garrison.

We were on the brink of war.

48

T HE COUNT RETURNED from Komneni's funeral even
more withdrawn than when he had left. Almost all
the lords of Arberia had gone to the ceremony, but apparently not even the sight of the old prince's coffin,
around which they were all gathered perhaps for the last
time, gave them the wisdom to finally reach an understanding among themselves.

Silence again reigned through all the days that followed. Still nobody else had crossed the bridge. One day
only some frightened sheep somehow found themselves
on it and tried to turn back, but were unable to do so.
The sheep wandered over the bridge while the terrified
shepherd brandished his crook on the bank, calling for
the ferryman to carry him across.

This was the only event of these days. A few blades of
grass sprouted among the piles of stone and sand left beside the bridge. They were the first sign that nature was
slowly, very slowly, but insistently preparing to erase
from the face of the earth every trace that bore witness to

the presence of workmen on the bank of the Ujana e Keqe.

The days were numb with cold, with a few motionless clouds in the distant sky, and silent, silent. No news came from anywhere. They said that in a very distant country they were building a great wall. Plague had struck central Europe again.

On the eleventh of the month of Michaelmas, I happened to make a tour of duty as far as the borders of our territories, to the very spot where the domain of the neighboring Turkish pasha begins. After completing my work, I would sit for hours on end, contemplating the point where the Turkish Empire began. I could not believe it was there in front of me. I repeated to myself over and over again, like someone wandering in his mind, that what they call the lands of Islam began a few paces in front of me. Asia began two paces in front of me. It was indeed enough to turn your wits. What had once been more distant than the lands of fairy tales was now in front of our very noses. And still I could not believe it. Nor could anybody believe that these people had really come so close. There they were, yet evidence, times, dates, and the units of measurement of time and space dissolved as if in a mist. Sometimes I wanted to call out: Where are they? Below, the land was the same, and the same winter sky covered the earth. And yet just here began, or rather ended, their enormous state, which began in the Chinese deserts.

I had seen nobody on the other side during the days of my tour of duty, neither guards nor inhabitants. There was only land left waste, more like a stony desert, and scrub everywhere. Only on the last night (oh, if only I had not stayed that night), on that final night I heard their music. I still do not know where that singing and accompaniment came from, who was singing, or why. I wonder whether they were wandering dervishes caught on the border as night fell, or civil servants sent from the capital to set border stones, or a group of itinerant musicians. In the end, I did not worry much about it. But when I heard their singing accompanied by entirely unfamiliar instruments, I felt seized by a sensation I had never known before. It was a diffused anxiety, without the slightest hint of hope. What was this stupor, this hashish dissolved in the air in the form of song? Its tones slithered drowsily; everything seemed sticky and shapeless. So this was their music, I thought, their inmost voice. It crept toward us like a soporific mist. At its tones, feet skipping in a dance would falter as if seized by terror.

I returned bitter and sour from my journey.

Nothing noteworthy happened until the middle of the month, apart from the appearance of the body of a drowned man floating one day on the surface of the waters. It collided with the pier where the body was immured (the water level had now risen this far), twirled around, and struck the pier once again with its elbow, as if to say to the dead man, How are you, brother? Then it floated away.

Those who had seen the drowned man and tried to tell other people were met with stares of incredulity. But that happened last year, people said. We saw it together. Don't you remember? And both sides would sit in bewilderment. By the bridge piers, time, swirling like water, seemed to have stood still.

49

O NE MORNING they woke me before dawn to tell me that people were crossing the bridge.

"Who?" I asked sleepily.

"The Baltaj family, all the men of the house together, with their black ox."

I went up to the narrow window-slit that overlooked the bridge. I knew that one day human beings would set foot on it, but I did not think it would happen so soon. By next spring at the earliest, I thought. Besides, I was also sure that some lone individual would be the first to dare, and not the Baltajs with a flock of children.

"Where are they going, I wonder? What has got into them?" I asked nobody in particular.

"No doubt some worry," called a voice from below.

Worry, I thought. What else could those black sheepskins contain?

The first sheepskin, the tallest of them, who was leading the ox, emerged at the opposite bank without suffering any harm. After him came the shorter ones, and finally the children.

"They crossed," somebody said.

They expected me to say something, perhaps a curse or, on the contrary, a blessing on the travelers. Perhaps they had felt a secret wish to cross the bridge for a long time. I had experienced something of this sort myself, and whenever I felt its pull I would walk to and fro for a long while, tiring my feet, as if this desire were simply in my feet alone, and I were punishing them for it.

So the Baltajs had crossed . . . only their menfolk. I remembered that in the villages, crossing the rainbow was considered so impossible that people thought that if girls went over they could be turned into boys. . . . And suddenly it flashed into my mind that nothing other than a rainbow must have been the first sketch for a bridge, and the sky had for a long time been planting this primordial form in people's minds. . . .

I felt afraid of all this hostility toward the bridge. However, I calmed myself at once. The divine model had been pure. But here, although the bridge pretended to embody this idea, it had death at its foundations.

The Baltajs, who had sold their black ox because of some problem, returned bitter and disconsolate, crossing the bridge again, but without their animal. Everybody talked about their crossing, but there was neither anger nor reproach in their words. There was only something like a sigh.

In the meantime Uk the ferryman had fallen ill. He had caught cold, which was not in itself something unexpected. But when it became known, everyone seemed to be astonished. Night and day on that dilapidated raft, his

151

feet in the water, forty and more years on end. How had he never caught cold before?

He died soon and was buried on the same day. It was a cloudy afternoon. The Ujana e Keqe was full of waves, and the blackened raft, moored to its jetty by chains, bucked on the waters like a furious horse that had sensed the death of its master.

"Boats and Rafts" did not replace the ferryman. It did not even remember the abandoned raft. The post that supported the sign with its name and the tolls was now very unsteady, and one day someone took it away.

As if the ferryman's death were some long-awaited sign, people one after another began to use the bridge. After the Baltajs, the Kryekuqe family crossed the bridge, and after them the landlord of the Inn of the Two Roberts, together with his brother-in-law, both drunk. On the same day some foreign travelers crossed, and at midday on the eighteenth of the month large numbers of the Stres clan passed over, a pregnant woman among them.

None of the Zenebishas crossed. There were also many old men and women, led by old Ajkuna, who had not only vowed never to commit the sin of setting foot on that devil's backbone but left instructions in their wills that even after their deaths they would prefer their coffins to be hurled into the water rather than carried over the bridge to the graveyard on the opposite bank.

Meanwhile, the abandoned raft tied by its chain to the old jetty rotted and crumbled in an extraordinarily short time. Such a thing was indeed surprising, especially when you think that the ferryman had made virtually no repairs for decades. People had only to give up using it for a very short while before it disintegrated.

50

O N THE THIRD OF THE MONTH of St. Ndreu, early in
the morning, Dan Mteshi crossed the bridge, together with his sons and a goat. After him, the men of the
Gjorg clan crossed on their way to the law court. Then
mad Gjelosh crossed (or rather advanced to the middle
and turned back). Later, all noise and laughter, almost the
entire Vulkathanaj clan crossed, mounted on mules, traveling to a wedding in Buzëzesta. Immediately afterward
Duda's daughters crossed, as did mad Gjelosh, making a
zigzag path. At midday two groups of strangers crossed
one after the other, and then a drunkard from the Inn of
the Two Roberts; then mad Gjelosh braced himself to set
off again but did not do so. Toward dusk, on his bay
mount, the knight Stanish Stresi crossed as fast as you
could blink, though nobody could say why, and after him
a foreign herald. When night fell crossings became very
rare, and anyway travelers were no longer recognizable in
the darkness. As their silhouettes appeared on the bridge,

you could gather a little from their gait, such as whether they were Albanians or foreigners, but there was no way that you could tell why they were traveling, whether for pleasure, penance, or murder.

51

N OT A LIVING SOUL crossed the bridge for one hundred hours in a row. Rain fell. The horizon was dissolved in mist. They said that plague was ravaging central Europe.

What was this interruption? For a time it seemed that people, having committed such a sin (and there were those who came to confession immediately after crossing the bridge), had made an agreement to abandon the bridge for good. However, on Sunday night the traffic resumed as unexpectedly as it had ceased.

When I was at leisure, I enjoyed choosing a sheltered spot and observing the bridge. The bridge was like an open book. As I watched what was happening on it, it seemed to me that I could grasp its essence. It sometimes seemed to me that human confidence, fear, suspicion, and madness were nowhere more clearly manifest than on its back. Some people stole over as if afraid of damaging it, while others thunderously stamped across it.

There were those who continued to cross at night,

bandit style, as if scared of somebody, or perhaps of the bridge itself, since they had spoken so ill of it.

After the bishop of Ardenica, who was traveling to defrock a priest at the Monastery of the Three Crosses, another covered wagon crossed, which, it was later suspected, probably contained an abducted woman. Then came oil traders. Mad Gjelosh followed the traders, shouting, because it was well known that he could not endure the seepages from their skin bottles. With a rag in his hand, he would stagger almost on his knees, wiping away the traces of oil, and with the same rag wiping the stone sides of the bridge, as if to clean them of dust.

Late in the afternoon there came, from who knows where, Shtjefen Keqi and Mark Kasneci, or Mark Haberi as he had recently begun to call himself. They had set off a week earlier with a great deal of fuss "to look death in the eye," but, it seemed, were coming back as always like drenched chickens.

Two months previously Mark Kasneci had caused us a great deal of confusion with his new surname. After a trip to the fiefdom of the Turkish pasha, he came back and announced that he was no longer called Mark Kasneci but Mark Haberi, which has the same meaning of "herald" in Turkish. He was the first person to change his surname, and people went in amazement to see him. He was the same as he always was, Mark Kasneci, the same flesh and bone, but now with a different name. I summoned him to the presbytery and said, "Mark, they say that along with your surname you have also changed your religion." But he swore to me that that was not true. When I told him that a surname was not a cap you could change whenever you liked, he begged me with tears in his eyes to forgive him and to let him come to church, be-cause, although he felt he was a sinner, he liked the sur-name so much and would not be parted from it. . . .

That is what people are like. It sometimes occurred to me that if the bridge were conscious, it would be more disgusted than amused by us and would take to its heels like a frightened beast. A rainbow, the bridge's model and perhaps its inspiration, is something that, thank God, no-body yet knows how to build, and still less to chain in fet-ters; but is it not also something frightening, fragile, and incomprehensible to people?

52

A T THE END OF THE WEEK the two representatives of
the bridge owners, mounted on mules, turned up
again after being absent for so long. People gaped at them
openmouthed when they arrived, as if they were seeing
shades. People's eyes followed them, as if asking, Still on
this earth?

They themselves did not show the slightest curiosity
in glancing at the bridge, not even at the dead man in the
first arch, but applied themselves immediately to the task
for which they had come. They dug two holes, one at the
entrance and the other at the end of the bridge, fixed iron
stakes in them, and fixed metal signs on the stakes, like
those that "Boats and Rafts" had once used. It was understood at once that these were tables of tolls for crossing the bridge. Everything was set out in detail; the toll
for individuals, reduced rates for whole families and
clans, the toll for the crossing of each head of livestock,
reductions for herds, the toll for individual carts, reductions for caravans, and so forth.

People looked at the sign as if to say, We turned our noses up before at crossing for free, and now we have to pay!

The two employees of the road and bridge company did not leave after erecting the signs but took over the ferryman's small abandoned lodge, which, it seems, the company had bought some time before. They began to do duty at the bridge in turns.

Surprisingly, people began to cross the bridge more and more often after the toll was imposed.

53

A VENETIAN MONK on his way to Byzantium brought more bad news from the Vlorë base. A Turkish imperial decree had just been issued, removing the base's old name of Orikum and renaming it Pasha-Lima. This was a terrifying and in any event an extraordinary name, since in Turkish it meant "port of ports," "chief port," or "pasha of ports." It was not hard to imagine what a military base with such a name would be used for. This was a great harbor opened by the Ottomans on Europe's very flank.

As the monk told me, Albanian and Turkish soldiers provoked each other daily at the boundary dividing the base. Dim-witted as he was, Balsha II could easily fall into a trap.

After the monk left, I went for a long walk on the banks of the Ujana e Keqe, and my thoughts were as murky as its waters. Time and again, that music of death I had heard weeks previously on the border came to my mind. Yes, they were trying to shackle our feet with that attenuated music. And after halting our dances they would bind our hands, and then our souls.

The hunger of the great Ottoman state could be felt in the wind. We were already used to the savage hunger of the Slavs. Naked and with bared teeth like a wolf's, this hunger always seemed more dangerous than anything else. But in contrast, the Ottoman pressure involved a kind of temptation. It struck me as no accident that they had chosen the moon as their symbol. Under its light, the world could be caressed and lulled to sleep more easily.

As I walked along the riverbank, this caress terrified me more than anything else. Dusk was falling. The bridge looked desolate and cold. And suddenly, in its slightly hunched length, in its arches and buttresses, and in its solitude, there was an expectancy. What are you waiting for, stone one? I said to myself. Distant phantoms? Or an imperial army and the sound of nameless feet, marching ten, twenty, a hundred hours without rest? Cursed thing.

54

N EWS FOLLOWED HARD ON NEWS, as frequent and grim as clouds in a dark season. The Turks had launched a major diplomatic offensive. More than half the Balkan peninsula was now under the Ottoman crescent. Three of the eleven lords of Arberia had also accepted vassalage. Throughout the Balkans, Turkish armies were on large-scale maneuvers in order to strike fear into those princes and dukes who still hesitated. The famous "Arbanon Line" of seven fortresses from Shkodër to Lezhë, which defended Byzantium from the Slavs, was crumbling. Byzantium itself had lost its vigor. The Balkan nobles — Albanians, Croats, Greeks, Serbs, Romanians, Macedonians, and Slovenes — sent their couriers sometimes to Venice and sometimes to Turkey, and sometimes in both directions simultaneously, to choose the lesser of the two dangers. They said that messengers left by one door, while at another entered drawers of straws and especially readers of shoulder blades, as people had recently called those who predict the approach or retreat of war by the color of a ram's shoulder blade. It is said that immediately after one dinner, at which the reader of the shoulder blade was horrified by the reddish tinge of the bone, the count of the Skurajs sent messengers to the sultan. The Muzakas were also wavering. The stand of the Dukagjins was unknown. They had withdrawn into the depths of the mountains, as they usually did at such times, and were brooding behind the mists. There is always time to die, their forebear had said. However, the phrase has been considered ambiguous; it is not clear which is considered death, the acceptance of war or of vassalage. They had never been sycophants, but nevertheless at such times you must prepare yourself for anything.

Increasingly I remembered their emblems, with all their lions' manes, fangs, claws, and cockspurs, as if to determine the stands they would take. . . . Just as often I remembered the laughter of the two countesses on the bank of the Ujana e Keqe, when they flirted with the name of "Abdullahth," and then their gossip about their sister-in-law Katrina, or "the queen" as they sarcastically called her, because her husband Karl Topia was a pretender to the long-vacant throne of Arberia. I remembered all these things and became as frightened of these dainty women as of the Turkish yataghan. I was frightened of the gifts and silks with which the Ottomans were so generous, and which the ladies coveted so much.

Some time ago, when the count of Kashnjet and the duke of Tepelenë had been the first to accept vassalage, they had mocked those who had predicted disaster. You said that the Turks would destroy us and strip us and disgrace us, they said. But we are still masters of our lands.

Our castles are still where they were; our coats of arms, our honor, and our possessions are untouched. If you don't believe us, come and see with your own eyes.

That is how they, and their ladies especially, wrote to other nobles. In fact it was true in a way. The Turk did not touch them. Nothing had changed, except for something that seemed tiny and unimportant. . . . This was the matter of the date at the head of their letters. Instead of the year 1378, they had written "*hijrah* 757," according to the Islamic calendar, the adoption of which was one of the Ottomans' few demands.

How unlucky they were. They had turned time back six hundred years, and they laughed and joked. How terrible!

55

N EVER BEFORE had so many travelers stayed at the
Inn of the Two Roberts. They also brought news,
most of it, alas, bleak.

The Muzakas had sent back the Ottomans' third deputation. The two barons Gropa and Matranga, on the
contrary, had declared their vassalage. So had two Serbian kings in the frontier regions and another Croatian
prince. It was not yet known what Nikollë Zaharia and
his vassals had decided, nor the Kastriotis. There were
whispers about an alliance between the two most powerful nobles, the great count Karl Topia and Balsha II, but
this could just as well be wishful thinking as the truth.
The question of the crown, to which Topia was a pretender, was an almost insuperable obstacle to such a pact.
Others said that Topia had sent his own messengers to
forge an alliance with the king of Hungary. As for old
Balsha, he had withdrawn to the mountains like the
Dukagjins, and besides, he was too old to lead a cam-

paign. Nevertheless, singly and in wretched isolation, some in twos or occasionally in threes, the majority of the Albanian nobles prepared for war. Count Stres, our liege lord, also called on all his vassals and knights to stand by.

We were on the brink of war, and only the blind could fail to see it. Since the Ottoman state became our neighbor, I do not look at the moon as before, especially when it is a crescent. No empire has so far chosen a more masterful symbol for its flag. When Byzantium chose the eagle, this was indeed superior to the Roman wolf, but now the new empire has chosen an emblem that rises far higher in the skies than any bird. It has no need to be drawn like our cross, or to be cut in cloth and hoisted above castle turrets. It climbs into the sky itself, visible to the whole of mankind, unhindered by anything. Its meaning is more than clear: the Ottomans will have business not with one state or two states, but with the whole world. Your flesh creeps when you see it, cold, with sometimes a honey-colored and sometimes a bloody tinge. Sometimes I think that it is already bemusing us all from above. There is a danger that one day, like sleepwalkers, we will rise to walk toward our ruin.

Last night as I prayed, I unconsciously replaced the words of the holy book, "Let there be light," with "Let there be Arberia!" almost as if Arberia had in the meantime been undone. . . .

I myself was terrified by this inner voice. Later, when I tried to discover from whence it came, I recalled all kind of discussions and predictions now being made about the future of this country. Arberia will find itself several times on the verge of the abyss. Like a falling stone, it will draw sparks and blood. It is said that it will be made and unmade many times before it stands fixed for all time on the face of the earth. So, let there be Arberia!

56

D ESPITE THE GREAT FROST, there are Turkish troop
movements on the border. The drums are inaudible,
but their banners can be discerned from a distance.

One morning, sentries of the principality appeared at
both ends of the bridge. Our liege lord's estrangement
from the neighboring pasha had deepened.

The armed guards remained at the bridge day and
night, next to the signs with the tolls. We thought this
must be a temporary measure, but after three days the
guards were not withdrawn but reinforced.

Dark news came from all sides. Old Balsha had gone
completely blind, night coming to his eyes before his soul.
As the saying goes, "May I not see what is to come!"

57

M EANWHILE, as if not caring about what was happening throughout the Balkans, travelers whose
road brought them this way, or rich men journeying to
see the world, paused more often at the bridge. This had
become so common recently that the landlord of the Inn
of the Two Roberts had placed a kind of notice at both
his gates, written in four languages: "For those guests de-
siring to see the famous Three-Arched Bridge, with the
man immured within, the inn provides outward and return journeys at the following rates . . ." (The tariff in
various currencies followed.)

A large cart drawn by four horses and equipped with
elevated seats carried the guests to and from the bridge
two or three times a day and sometimes more often.
Loudmouthed and boorish, as idle travelers usually are,
they swarmed around and under the bridge, noticing
everything with curiosity, touching the piers, crouching
under the approach arches, and lingering by the first arch
where the man was immured. Their polyglot, monoto-

nous, and interminable chatter took over the site. I went among them several times to eavesdrop on this jabbering, which was always the same and somehow different from the previous day's. The flow of time seemed to have stood still. They talked about the legend and the bridge, asked questions and sought explanations from each other, confused the old legend with the death of Murrash Zenebisha, and tried to sort matters out but only confused them further, until the cart from the inn arrived, bringing a fresh contingent of travelers and taking away the previous one. Then everything would start again from the beginning. "So this whole bridge was built by three brothers?" "No, no, that's what the old legend says. This was built by a rich man who also surfaces roads and sells tar. He has his own bank in Durrës." "But how was this man sacrificed here, if it's all an old legend?" "I think there is no room for misunderstanding, sir. He sacrificed himself to appease the spirits of the water, and in exchange for a huge sum in compensation paid to his family." "Ah, so it was a question of water spirits; but you told me it had no connection with the legend." "I'm not saying it has no connection, but . . . the main thing was the business of the compensation."

And then they would begin talking about the compensation, whistling in amazement at the enormous sum, calculating the percentages the members of his family would earn from the bridge's profits, and converting the sums into the currencies of their own principalities, and then into Venetian ducats. And so, without anyone noticing, the conversation would leave the bridge behind and concentrate on the just-arrived news from the Exchange Bank in Durrës, particularly on the fluctuating values of various currencies and the fall in the value of gold sovereigns following the recent upheavals on the peninsula. And this would continue until some traveler, coming late to the crowd, would say: "They seemed to tell us that it was a woman who was walled up, but this is a man. They even told us that we would see the place where the milk from the poor woman's breast dripped." "Oh," two or three voices would reply simultaneously, "Are you still thinking of the old legend?"

And it would all go back again to the beginning.

58

I T WAS MARK HABERI who was the first to bring the news of the Turks' "commination" against Europe from across the border. Pleased that the event seemed so important to me, he looked at me with eyes that reminded me of my displeasure at his change of surname, almost as if, without that Turkish surname, he would not be able to bring news, in other words *habere,* from over there.

Indeed, his explanation of what had happened was so involved that while he talked, he became drenched with sweat, like a man who fears to be taken for a liar. Speak clearly, I said to him two or three times, because I cannot understand what you are trying to say. But he continued to prevaricate. I can't say it, he repeated. These are new, frightening things that cannot be put into words.

He asked for my permission to explain by gestures, making some movements that struck me as demented. I told him that the gesture he was making is among us called a "fig," and indicates at the same time contempt, indifference, and a curse. He cried, "Precisely, Father. There they call it a 'commination,' and it is of state importance."

I did not conceal my amazement at the connection between this hand movement, which people and especially women make in contempt of each other, somewhat in the sense of "may my ill fortune be on your head," with the new Ottoman state policy toward Europe, of which Mark Haberi sought to persuade me.

He left in despair to collect additional data, which he indeed brought me a few days later, always from the other side. They left me openmouthed. From his words and the testimony of others that I heard in those days, I reconstructed the entire event, like a black temple.

The Commination against Europe had taken place in the last days of the month of Michaelmas, precisely on the Turkish-Albanian border, and had been performed according to all the ancient rubrics in the archives of the Ottoman state. Their rules of war demanded that before any battle started, the place about to be attacked, whether a castle, a wall, or simply an encampment, had to be cursed by the army's curse maker.

It was said that the old archives described precisely, even with the help of a sketch, the gesture of the curse. The palms of the hand were opened and moved forward, as if to launch the portentous curse on its flight. This gesture was repeated three times, and then the curser's back was turned on the direction in which the curse was headed.

Their chronicles told of the cursing of castles and the domains of rebellious pashas, and even whole states, before an attack began; but there was no case of an entire continent being cursed. It was perhaps for this reason that even the most important curse maker in the state, Sukrullah, who had arrived on the empire's extreme border the previous night, was slightly shaken, as those who saw him reported.

The sky was overcast and damp, and the whole plain around the small temporary minaret erected specially for the purpose was swathed in mist.

The curse maker climbed the little minaret and stared for a while in our direction, toward where, in Turkish eyes, the accursed continent of Europe began. The weather was indeed extremely bad, and almost nothing could be seen in the fog. The small group of high dignitaries who had accompanied Sukrullah from the capital to the border stood speechless. Down below, at the foot of the minaret, the imperial chronicler had opened a thick tome to record the event.

Sukrullah raised his arms in front of him, so that they emerged from the wide sleeves of his half-clerical, half-laic gown. Everybody saw that the palms of his hands were exceptionally broad. However, nobody was surprised at this, because he was not the state's foremost curse maker for nothing.

He studied his hands for a while and, turning his eyes toward the ash-colored distance, raised his palms in front of his face to the level of his brow. His palms paled as the blood drained from them. He held them there for a time until they were as white as the palms of a corpse, and then thrust them violently forward, as if the evil were in the form of a bubble he was dispatching into the distance.

He did this three times in a row. The commination was complete.

In silence, without a word, he climbed down first from the minaret, followed immediately by his escorts. Together with the other officials, they accompanied him to his carriage, whose doors were embellished with the emblem of the Great Royal Commination. He climbed into the carriage together with his assistants and guards, and as the vehicle departed through the winter cold in the direction from which it had come, the curse traveled in the opposite direction, toward us, toward the lands of Europe. It went (or rather came) through the fog like some bird of ill omen, like a herald or a sick dream.

So, God on high, there it is! What sort of country is this with which fate has embroiled us? What signs it sends through the air to us! And what will it send after them?

59

T HE MONTH OF ST. NDREU began and ended in fog. Sometimes the fog seemed to freeze stock-still. Everything half dissolved in it: the riverbanks, the nearby hamlets, the bleak sandbank, the bridge. On such days of mist the victim immured in the lap of the bridge seemed both more remote and closer, as if he would shortly resolve his ambiguous position and step out toward us, a living man toward the living, or retreat, a dead man toward the dead.

But he remained in between, neither in this world nor in the next, a constant burden to us all. Nobody knew what had happened to his flesh inside, but his plaster mask was still the same. His open, vacant eyes, his cheeks, lips, and chin, were the same as before. Sometimes a drop of moisture would appear on his features, as if on the surface of a wall, and leave a mark when it dried.

There were people who stayed for a long time, trying to decipher these signs. There were noisy crowds who chattered under his very nose, shook their fingers in front of his eyes, and even criticized him. Anybody else suspended in his position would not dream of anything but gathering his own bones in some grave. It was believed that lightning frightened him, while ravens no longer flew low above him.

His family's visits became rarer. They now no longer came in two hostile groups, but in four: his wife and baby, his parents, and his two brothers separately. Their quarrel over sharing the compensation had deepened during the autumn, and the lawsuit they had initiated over its division would be, it seemed, hopelessly protracted.

Each party came and stayed a while by the plaster mask as if before a court, with their own explanations and worries. The man's open eyes stared at them all impartially, while the visitors no doubt imagined that next time they would reach a better understanding with the plaster.

Next time . . . There were indeed days on which it seemed that he would surmount the plaster barrier and would give to them and take from them. It would be his turn to judge perhaps not only his relatives but people of all kinds.

I have seen statues age, but my mind tells me that this bas-relief, perhaps the only one in the world with the dead man's flesh, bones, and maybe soul inside it, will have a different life expectancy. Either it will burst prematurely, or it will outlive all others. The seasons will deposit their dust on it, the wind will slowly, very slowly erode it, as it erodes all the world, and he, Murrash Zenebisha, who has now donned his protective mask, and for whom the years have stopped, will eventually find old age. But old age will come not by years and seasons, in the normal way of human age, but by centuries. Sometimes I say to myself, Poor you, Murrash Zenebisha. What horrors you will see. For the future seems to me pregnant only with terrible disasters. But sometimes I think to myself, You are fortunate in what you will see, because, whatever will happen, I am sure that like every storm this too will pass, just as every night finds a dawn.

60

THE BLOODSHED occurred one day before Christmas, at four in the afternoon. Everything took place in a very short time, the bat of an eyelid, but it was an event of the kind that is able to divide time in two. Since that day in the month of St. Ndreu, people do not talk about time in general, they talk about time before and time after.

Until shortly before four o'clock (on that cloudy day, it seemed to have been four o'clock since morning), until just before the fatal moment, there was no ominous sign anywhere. Everything looked empty, when suddenly, God knows how, the chill fog spawned seven horsemen. They were approaching at speed with a curious kind of gallop, not in a straight line but describing wide arcs, as if an invisible gale were driving their horses first in one direction and then in another. When they drew near enough to distinguish their helmets and breastplates, they were seen to be Turkish horsemen.

When our sentries on the right bank saw that the

horsemen were coming to the bridge, they blocked the entrance with crossed spears. The horsemen continued their rush toward the bridge in their unusual gallop, describing arcs. Our sentries made signs for them to halt. They were required to stop, even if they had crossed the border with permission, and all the more so if they had come without permission, which had often happened recently. But the horsemen did not obey.

To those who witnessed the skirmish from the distance of the riverbank, it resembled a dumb show. Two of the Turkish horsemen were able to rush through our guards and head for the middle of the bridge. A third was brought down from his mount, and a skirmish began around him. One of our guards ran after the horsemen who were racing ahead. Those left behind, Albanians and Turks, crossed spears. Another horseman succeeded in struggling free of the confusion and went on the heels of our guard, who was pursuing the first two horsemen. Meanwhile, our sentries on the left side of the bridge were rushing to the help of their comrades. They met the first two Turkish horsemen in the center of the bridge. An Albanian sentry pursuing the horsemen joined the fight, as did the third Turkish rider, who had pursued our guard.

Yet all this happened, as I said, in total silence, or seemed to, because the raging of the river smothered every sound. Only once (ah, my flesh creeps even now when I think of it), did a voice emerge from the dumb tumult. It was no voice, it was a broken *kra*, a horrible cry from some nonhuman throat. And then that play of shadows again, with somebody running from the middle of the bridge to the right bank, and returning to rescue someone who had fallen. There was a clash of spears, and at last the repulse of the horsemen, and their retreat into the fog out of which they had come, with one riderless horse following them, neighing.

That was all. The horizon swallowed the horsemen just as it had given them birth, and you could have thought they were only a mirage, but . . . there was evidence left at the bridge. Blood stained the bridge at its very midpoint.

The count himself soon came to the scene of the incident. He walked slowly across the bridge, while the guards, their breastplates scarred with spear scratches, told him what had happened. They paused by the pool of blood. It must have been the blood of the Turkish soldier, whose body the horsemen had succeeded in recovering. As the blood froze, the stones of the gravel made its final gleam more visible.

"Turkish blood," our liege lord said in a hoarse, broken voice.

Nobody could tear his eyes away. We had seen their Asiatic costume. We had heard their music. Now we were seeing their blood . . . the only thing they had in common with us.

This day was bound to come. It had long been traveling in the caravan of time. We had expected it, but perhaps not so suddenly, with those seven horsemen emerging from the mist and being swallowed by the mist again, followed by a loose horse.

61

THE MORE THE HOURS PASSED, the more serious the incident appeared. Nightfall enlarged its significance in an extraordinary way. So did the days that followed. The silence that fell the following week, far from diminishing its importance, heightened it yet further. Those movements on the bridge that seemed from a distance like the dance of madmen were repeated in everybody's minds in slow motion, as if in delirium. It was like a first sketch for war. It was obvious now that this had not been a chance patrol. From the base at Vlorë to the mountains of the Dukagjins and the Kastriotis, the Turks had sparked off a series of provocations. You would have had to have less sense than mad Gjelosh not to realize that war had begun.

On Sunday, as I walked late at night on the deserted sandbank (the idiot had wandered cackling over the bridge a short time before), I felt a debility I had never experienced before. The moonlight fell evenly over the plain, freezing everything into a mask. Everything was wan; everything was dead, and I almost cried out: How can you become part of Asia, you, my lovely Arberia?

My eyes darkened, and just as I had seen that pale patch of blood under Murrash Zenebisha's neck, so it seemed to me that now, under that moonlight, I saw whole plains awash with blood, and mountain ranges burned to ash. I saw Ottoman hordes flattening the world and creating in its place the land of Islam. I saw the fires and the ash and the scorched remains of men and their chronicles. And our music, and dances, and costume, and our majestic language, harried by that terrible *"-luk,"* like a reptile's tail, seeking refuge in the mountains among the lightning and the beasts, which will turn it savage. And below the mountains, I saw the plains left without speech. And above all I saw the long night coming in hours, for centuries . . .

Unconsciously I had reached the bridge's first arch, where the immured man was. The moon illuminated him shockingly, and for a long time I stood there stunned, my gaze fixed on his plaster eyes. I was cold, as if he were conveying to me the iciness of the next world. "Murrash Zenebisha," I said silently. (The thought that I was imitating mad Gjelosh, who once used to talk to the dead man like this, did not worry me in the least.) "Murrash Zenebisha," I repeated, "You died before me, but will live after me. . . ." I could not muster the strength to tear my gaze away from those quenched eyes, whose whiteness was becoming unendurable. Why had I come here? What did I want to tell him, and what did I expect of him? I should have run as fast as I could from the splashing of the moonlight and from that place of sacrifice, but my legs failed me. At any moment it seemed that the curtain of plaster would fall from the dead man's eyes, allowing his message to pass. I could almost understand that message. We two are very close, monk, his eyes seemed to say. Do you not feel it?

I did indeed feel it precisely, and as I moved backward without taking my eyes from him (for this seemed the only way to break away from him), I felt I should return to the presbytery as soon as I could to complete my chronicle. I should return as soon as possible and finish it, because times are black; soon night may fall, it will be too late for everything, and we may pay with our lives for writing such testimonies. This was the immured man's message. And this chronicle, like the bridge itself, may demand a sacrifice, and that sacrifice can be none other than myself, *I, the monk Gjon, sonne of Gjorg Ukcama, who hath finyshed this knowynge that ther is no thynge wryttene in owre tonge about the Brigge of the Ujana e Keqe and the euil whyche is upon us, and for the love of owre worlde.*

Tiranë, 1976–1978